The Pendant
Part One

Anna Woodbridge

The Pendant

Author: Anna Woodbridge

First Published in 2025

ISBN 978-1-915996-42-8 (Paperback)
     978-1-915996-43-5 (E-Book)

Book Cover and Book Layout by:
     White Magic Studios
     www.whitemagicstudios.co.uk

Published by:
     Maple Publishers
     Fairbourne Drive, Atterbury,
     Milton Keynes,
     MK10 9RG, UK
     www.maplepublishers.com

A CIP catalogue record for this title is available from the British Library.

To my wonderful family, my fabulous Big Man, and my darling Binny. Thank you all for your support and love. You mean the world to me.

Time Line

Prologue – The Present

Do something Anna, *before it's too late.*

The fridge hummed in the background as the kettle breathed its last steamy breath into the air. Piles of scruffy, out of date magazines graced the old wooden table, crisscrossed with the scars of lunch battles over possibly, decades. I could feel the tension in the air, almost breathe it in.

There was a part of me that knew what was coming sensed it in the stale air, but I still hoped that today wasn't the day. I straightened my tense shoulders: *please don't let it be today, I'm not up to it, let it be tomorrow, … any tomorrow.*

I turned to her slowly, a casual smile on my lips, pretending I didn't have a clue.

"So …?" she said eventually, tilting her head to the side in a questioning way, stir, stir, stirring that coffee. Nothing else, just that. Very cool, very focussed, but it was the calmness in her tone that finally alerted me, it was so very unlike her, she of no patience whatsoever, I could practically taste her seething frustration.

The hairs on my arms stood to attention as I looked back at her carefully, aiming for an expression of amused but patient disinterest as I shook my head at her questioningly, a slight, fake, smile playing on my lips. "What?" I said, "What's up?"

"For Christ's sake, *come on* Anna," she hissed suddenly, making me jump and shocking me with the harshness of her tone, "bloody *talk* to me." I narrowed my eyes, pseudo quizzically, but she was there in an instant, cutting off my unformed words, shutting me down; "Nope, oh no … no, no, no, that doesn't cut it, Sis, not *this* time, it really doesn't, I'll just say these words, just, these, words, so listen, *we need to know*, do you hear me?" Her eyes locked on mine; We ***need*** to know, and you … you are going to *bloody, damn* well tell us!" She gathered herself to her full height, "Got it, sis? Spill … or there is going to be really, stupendously, big, fat, buggering trouble. I promise you that."

Elsie's breath hitched sharply, even as she reached out to touch my arm comfortingly; she'd shocked both of us with her words, her tone. I looked down at her hand, buying time, my lips working helplessly, trying to form the fabrications, because I still wasn't sure if this was the time, the right time anyway.

Her usually laughter filled brown eyes, drilled into mine unrelentingly, and just as I opened my mouth to speak, I was saved by the distant sound of the lunchtime bell. Thank you, dear Lord, I thought weakly. Catching a glimpse of her raised eyebrows and hearing her hiss of breath escape in frustrated exasperation, I whispered soothingly albeit a little bit too quickly, "Come round later, we can chat, ok?" and not waiting for an answer, I turned away, my palms clammy, damn them and I left her standing there, silent, watching me go.

Chapter 1 – The Present – Lorentree Cottage

And so here I was, sitting in Lorentree Cottage, the lamps on with the fire dancing, and the radio crooning gently in the background, sipping, aka *downing*, a vodka and tonic, and wondering how on earth I was going to start this conversation with my sisters. I shifted guiltily; fingers cramped from gripping the glass too tightly. Jon and me were the eldest, the only ones for the first eight years of my life, this was a conversation I should have with him present, to help me.

The sudden rap on the door made me jump and jolted me out of my thoughts, heralding the arrival of Elsie and Libby. Windswept, fresh and damp from the darkness, they stampeded into the front room, bringing a sense of untamed expectancy and restrained excitement. They also brought Prosecco and Rioja, God bless them, and some fabulously indulgent Cornish brie. Alongside "I'm not taking these boots off" and "Christ that bloke next door is bloody nosey" they finally managed to grab a glass each, gleefully open up the cheese and biscuits, loading the coffee table, before snuggling feet up on the old, voluminous sofa, expectation written clearly across their faces.

"Well, tell us, Sis," Elsie demanded immediately. "I only get out once a month, so this better be good, the bus was rank." She smiled winningly all the same and pushed her dark curls off her face, sniffing at her wine appreciatively. Libby was blond, a tad quieter, but she could easily liven up a room.

"What's going on Sis?" she asked quietly, "come on spill." Her blue eyes held mine gently. Had it ever happened that they'd both received a big sister 'summons' to Lorentree Cottage without knowing why before? No wonder their interest was piqued.

All this time and still I wasn't ready, not yet. I needed to think, just to plan an opener. I brushed my hair off my face, flustered. I didn't know how to start the conversation. It didn't matter how many times I'd practised, the light hearted approach:

"Hey you'll never guess," the "Look I know it's crazy"; the "I've something to tell you …" well, the words all seemed so flippant. Secrets, kept, no not just kept, guarded was a better word, from two of my favourite people. Two people who trusted me with all their secrets, even the embarrassing ones. I sighed heavily feeling my mood plunge even lower. I wouldn't be able to talk my way out of my reasons for keeping this quiet, it was such a huge part of all our lives, and maybe there wasn't an explanation good enough for having withheld this information at all, let alone for so long.

I sighed deeply; I was afraid. Afraid I would lose them, afraid of their reactions, terrified perhaps even more, that they wouldn't believe me. I swallowed dryly, my mouth like the desert, I felt alone, and so inadequate for the task in hand. Even Lorentree Cottage seemed to be waiting, reaching to comfort me in its warm embrace, trying to soothe me, while the fire whispered its graceful support, 'go on' it hissed, fluttering gently *'tell them'*.

Their attention held still, they looked at me questioningly, and the playfulness left them. I could practically see it get up and trot right out the front door, glad to be out of it. Suddenly I realised they must be worried, I had left them thinking that some dreadful thing, maybe a diagnosis, maybe news of a death, would be coming out of my lips. For God's sake, what was I like? I hastily gabbled out, "Hey you two, don't worry, it's not bad news, not like dying news or anything, it's absolutely …." And I caught the flow of emotions on their faces, relief, curiosity, concern, finally puzzlement.

"Well, what?" Elsie leant forward, at the same time as Libby, both leaning to comfort me in whatever mess I found myself in, such beautiful girls, so kind.

"I have this secret." I breathed out raggedly, I realised I'd forgotten to catch my breath for a while. Straightening my tension ridden shoulders, I continued, "I've had it a long, long time." I looked down in shame. "I've always wanted to tell you, please remember that, but the time was never right. At least I thought it was never right. You may both feel differently." I spoke slowly now, "Please don't hate me for not telling you earlier. This is not a story, or a … a prank, I really need you with me on this, ok?" My voice had lowered to a bit of a nervous whisper by the time I managed to get the words out of my mouth. There was silence while they both looked at me uneasily, but patiently.

"Go on, Sis," Libby said gently, "just tell us." They glanced at each other half puzzled, half exasperated with me.

"Whatever it is, it can't be that bad," said Elsie, very patiently for her, "no one's died," but her words fizzled out and she looked into my eyes as she whispered: "They really haven't, have they"?

"No," I answered again. "Really, no, they haven't." I think by this time they were too scared to find out what I had to tell them and before I could speak, Libby broke the strangled silence, "Well sod it, I need a smoke," she said darkly, as if her habit were all down to me. Shakily she reached into her bag, dragging out her baccy pouch. "I think you'll find it's better out than in," she said looking at me steadily and her calm blue eyes, held my gaze, "It's going to be ok; nothing is as bad as you think, let me have this," she said pointing with her rollie, "and we'll sort it all out." She made her way across the flagstones to the front door, and with a rush of cold air disappeared into the darkness.

"Flipping heck, Sis, that's how you milk a moment, what's going on?" Elsie asked. I glanced at her worriedly: "Wait until Libby's back, you both need to know, I can't tell you without her here." And as the clock ticked, we waited silently.

"Jon's here," was the so welcome shout as she came back in the door a few minutes later, tossing her blond hair over her shoulder. "He's parking. I didn't know he was coming over too?" Libby looked at me speculatively, I could see her very essence reaching to me to stroke my brow, comfort me, Libby was a healer. And she didn't know. Yet. I smiled at her fondly, "Yes, I asked him. I thought he might get here too late, but this is good, it's better." It was always better when Jon was around. He was a …., but no, first things first.

And in he came, my larger-than-life brother, the kindest of souls. Oh, he could make you laugh, deep endless belly laughs, but never at you, always alongside you; he made you feel you were the most important person at the table. I glanced up at him, and he looked right back at me, testing the air, gathering the vibe, smelling the atmosphere, a lifelong habit. I knew that, but I also knew it was more. "Well?" he said. "Is it the witches of Eastwick in here?" and they all chuckled, alongside a 'charming bruv!' and I glanced at him warning him with my eyes.

I put another log on the wood burner, filled up our glasses and we all settled down to the comfortable sound of the logs crackling and the clock ticking. Vaguely, the outside world intruded in the form of a door slamming in the distance, a tractor wending its way along the lane and the wind rattling against the front door of Lorentree Cottage, but they waited patiently, my precious siblings, for me to tell them my secret.

My hands were shaking and damp, I wiped them on my legs and gazed at them all, and they looked back fondly, almost as if they were waiting for the punch line of an office story. Prepared to laugh at my silly antics, something I had done to show myself up, I could see them getting the words ready to tell me that everyone else was at fault, not me; that it had been perfectly acceptable to have done the ridiculous thing I had done … again. So supportive, I felt a swell of love for them and their unerring care and, gulp, pre-emptive forgiveness. I sighed deeply.

"Okay …" I started, "when I was around six, I found out something about myself. Something I could do, something …. unusual." Full stop, I made myself wait, my fingers and toes practically twisting themselves into anxious, cramped knots. I swallowed and looked around at them …

"Look, it's probably best if I tell you what happened then, right from the start, it's a long story, are you ok to stay a while?" They nodded in turn, patiently.

Chapter 2 – 1968 – School

I hardly felt the wire cutting into my fingers, as I pressed myself up against the fence. My skin was wind burnt, smarting, as the cold air chafed meanly against my cheeks. I didn't care, not one bit. I was so desperately unhappy; I was drenched in tears and a fair bit of green tinged snot. Not my best look, and even at nearly five years old, and on my first day at big school I knew I wasn't helping myself. I wanted my Mum, I wanted to be at home with her, with my little brother Jon, with the fire going in the sitting room and Crown Court on the tele. I rubbed my knitted sleeve across my nose, smearing the snot across my cheek, and sniffed thickly in misery.

When I looked up a lone figure in a blue woollen coat was walking down the hill on the path opposite the school. Squinting into the weak October sunshine, I saw through puffy, tear-filled eyes that it was one of the dinner ladies, Mrs Brewster, probably on her way to the village shop. She was nice, I liked her, she was kind. The sight of a familiar face comforted me for a moment and I hoped that she would stop, maybe see me crying and take me home to Mum.

"Hello sweetheart," she said, smiling kindly, and stopping by the fence she swapped her shopping basket onto her other arm and offered me a clean tissue out of her coat pocket. "Are those tears I can see? Come on now, wipe that pretty little face and take a big breath. That's it, that's better." She reached a gloved finger through the wire and stroked my cold cheek. "Do you know, I bet all of your new friends are waiting for you to play with them, look at them all over there." She pointed to a group of equally desolate children standing in solitary, miserable aloneness, at the other side of the playground. Not one whose name I knew. "Why don't you see who's feeling sad, I bet you can cheer them up." Her gentle grey eyes twinkled at me. "It's hardly any time until Mum comes to pick you up, and then you can tell her all about your first day at school and who you played with." She looked at me expectantly.

It wasn't enough though, not nearly enough: "Please will you tell Mum to come and get me?" I said shakily, "I w-want to go h-home." I waited anxiously for her reply, my breath painful and uneven. "Well," she said brightly, but firmly, "I'm going straight down the shop now, and if I see Mum on her way to pick you up, I'll ask her to come double quick. How's that?" Kindness oozed from her. I gazed back, unbending my stiff fingers from the fence and turning away; it was not the result I wanted but I mumbled resignedly over my shoulder, "'S ok," as another warm, fat tear rolled down my face.

All that week I was utterly miserable. Every teatime when Mum was trying to chat to me about school, about my teacher Mrs MacDerwin, who was in truth exceedingly kind and comforting as well as enthusiastic and playful, I lowered my head, my eyes downcast and refused to speak. I decided to keep up the silent tactics until they took me seriously. I was double, double, sure that they would soon realise that big school was not for me when it upset me so much. I knew that Mum was worried and I felt a little bit mean, but I knew she really wanted me to stay home with her, after all I was her special big girl.

My hopes came to nothing when crouching beside the sitting room door that night in my nightie, eavesdropping and freezing my toes off, I heard Mum tearfully explaining to Dad how hard I was finding big school and how awful she felt for me, only to hear Dad say: "Well, unfortunately, Katarina, she's going to have to get used to it, we don't have choices about going to school." He gentled his tone "She'll be absolutely fine, darling, she'll make a little friend soon, you'll see. Look, I'll take her in tomorrow and we'll go to the park on Saturday, she'll love that, okay?" I listened out for Mum to argue, but no such luck. My heart sank into my slippers, and shoulders drooping, clutching my Beanie Boy, I stumbled back up to bed, feeling cold and hopeless.

Would you believe it? After a horrible sleepless night, tears before breakfast, sobs outside school, and being forcibly removed from my Dad's trousered leg, things started to look up and the day began to improve.

There was a new starter in Mrs MacDerwin's class and the little dark- haired, pretty, elfin child, felt like the friend I had been waiting for, for all of my nearly five years.

Everything changed almost overnight. When once my days had felt like an utter misery, a torment to be endured, where even the brushing of my blond curls had somehow seemed too painful to tolerate, such was the extent of my misery, well now, getting ready for my new school day, playing with plasticine together, practising our hymns and even drinking our cold, full fat milk, became a joyous experience. The two of us giggling together, sharing our packed lunches, swapping our crayons, our blond and dark heads touching as we made our little potions with dead leaves, worms and water in the playground, became part of every day.

Each evening I chatted tirelessly to Mum and Dad at teatime, ruling officiously over my poor little brother, supercilious and self-important with, "No Jon, you aren't big enough, you don't go to school" and "Jon can't do it, he's just a baby." Evie, my new and very *bestest* friend, had transformed my life.

Chapter 3 – 1969 – The Beginning

She looked at me really sadly, her eyes filling with unshed tears, that I knew she wouldn't allow to fall. "I don't mind," she whispered. "It's okay Anna." She was so sad, and there she was comforting me.

We were sitting on the hard chairs in the Prattern Hut, not far from the main school building. As the old Victorian school was too small for the blooming population of the village, a temporary classroom had been erected. We were auditioning in front of Mrs Williams for the Christmas Nativity and all the other children, in varying states of high energy and excitement had been asked to watch, and choose who they thought the best Mary would be. Mary had to be *'confident, speak clearly, and be willing to learn her lines'*.

Everyone had been given a part, but the Mary part was *very* sought after, and with a view to fairness Mrs Williams, who was the year 2 teacher, and also the headmaster's wife, had asked the children to watch all the auditions and vote on who they believed would do the role, full justice. Fenella had won the vote, mostly because her of her favouritism with the boys, who admired her four-minute sprint around the playground, while still continuing to appear as though she had a gallon of breath left in her willowy *'clever dick, I can't do anything wrong, Fennelly the Smelly'* body.

"Her hair is long and black; she looks a bit like Mary." Evie continued bravely, her eyes wet, but the extent of her disappointment, epic in our young lives, was on the scale of the Titanic going down, and I was under no illusion how deeply she was disappointed. I was resentful and crosser on my best friend's behalf than I had ever been. Her audition had been really good, I could just punch those *stupid* boys.

I was very happy with my role of the Angel Gabriel and with my blond curls, I was probably an ideal choice. Also, I could chuck my voice right across the Church, watching it soar its way right over to Mum and Dad, and even hold Jon in his chair in ear splitting awe. I completely understood Evie's train of thought regarding the colour and length of Mary's hair, but it didn't stop me feeling protective and upset that *Fennelly the Smelly* had landed the prime role. Fenella was okay, but she was already clever, already spoilt even if she was still a tiny bit nice. She already had long hair, which was very, very shiny, and in all honesty, she also didn't much look like she was either pleased or surprised about getting the class vote to play the main role. Even when she got out of school, she'd forget to tell her Mum she'd landed the leading part, you could just bet on it!

Really all I did was wish it was different, I wished very fervently indeed, with a good degree of righteous indignation involved, that Evie had got the part of Mary. I was just imagining in my head how she would look in Mary's blue and white dress, with her dark curls, how well she would say her lines, nice and loud, holding her head up so her voice went flying to all the Mums and Dads, oh and she would hold that baby doll that Mrs Williams had brought in really carefully and gently; she was great at pretending she had her own baby.

I thought to myself, how her dark hair and elfin build would look brilliant beside Joseph who was sturdy and wholesome, who both of us thought was good boyfriend material because of his dark, curly eyelashes, and then out of nowhere, I just got this dreadful headache in my ears, all of a sudden. I put small, shaky hands up to clutch at my head, to cover my aching ears, and as I did, I could see flashing scenes in front of my eyes: Evie, looking sad, eyes full of unshed tears, Fenella auditioning, Mrs Williams talking us through our lines, asking us to make our voices fly, Joseph silently mouthing his stilted words, me, pretending to be the Angel Gabriel, loud but careful so my words were clear, like Mum said, and then… then it all just stopped, absolutely stopped.

All the flitting scenes stopped, and for a split second there was nothing but darkness, pitch black, darkness. Like I'd gone blind. And then the scenes started again.

But this time they started just at the end of the auditions, a moment before the roles were going to be cast, and I watched in silent confusion, my head spinning, my ears still aching like glory, as the children voted for Evie … for *Evie* to be Mary.

Chapter 4 – 1976 – River Meadow Cottage

"Can I wear my pink t-shirt pees?" Elsie asked plaintively. She knew very well that she had worn it for two days in a row and the washing turnaround in a two-bedroom cottage, with six of us living there was a haphazard, lucky if you ever got a sock to match, process, and a '*it's just not going to happen for two more days sweetheart*'. I sighed, "Elsie it's dirty, you know it is, you can't keep wearing it day after day, it needs to be washed." I stroked her dark curls and she looked up at me with big brown eyes, that is in fact, all she did, and I knew that it was going to be a headache moment once again. "But you can *made* it clean, Anna," she wheedled pressing her small hand into mine, "peeeeees?"

Jon and I were now two sisters up, we had Elsie, born in 1971 who was five years old, quirky and funny with delicious dark curls and brown eyes. She could wrap us around her little finger without even speaking, and Libby, with beautiful big blue eyes and blond hair, she looked almost fey, as though she was too fragile to be part of this rough and tumble world, how could you not spoil her, protect her, born in 1973 and three years old. She was already the kindest child.

"Elsie, I just don't need this, you know how my head hurts sometimes when you ask me for things that you shouldn't, things that you don't really need." I looked down at her gravely, willing her to give in on the pink, bloody t-shirt thing she had going on, but one glance at her mutinous face and quivering lip, had me dragging in a breath and turning to find a space, any space at all in fact, to try and *'made it clean'* for her.

"Anna?" Mum stopped me in my tracks, appearing out of nowhere, which in itself was tricky in a cottage this size, and looking at me with raised eyebrows, hands tucked into her pinny pockets, said, "What are you doing sweetheart?" Her voice was calm, questioning, maybe a little hesitant, but I couldn't read her.

I gazed back at her; a slim, pretty, blonde haired, woman, loving and straight talking. Always ready to laugh. But not now, now she waited silently for my answer.

Shit, I thought wordlessly, flustered, what now? I swallowed heavily, what was she *really* asking me, was she really questioning anything other than *'what was I doing today, right now, was I busy?'* I wasn't sure, I just couldn't judge how much she was aware of, did she know anything at all, had she seen something? I thought back: I had been so careful, always alone, usually away from River Meadow Cottage, mostly at night or at the very least hidden. If she suspected anything, and even more importantly, if she was suspicious, how much did she actually *want* to know … or … *bloody hell*, need to know?

I scraped my hand through my tangled, unruly curls buying a moment, and in a split second of recognition, I knew what she needed. I knew that she needed everything to be ordinary, normal and safe. She needed everything she already had, everything she understood, all the ups and downs of life in a house bulging with her children, tons of love to wrap us all up in and keep us safe; she needed a straightforward life with boundaries she understood. She needed all that, because that's what she had bought into, what her life's guidelines were, what her days, weeks, months and years were supposed to be, and that's what she deserved. And I would damn well make sure that's what she got, because I loved her, and because I wanted that for her too.

The angel on my shoulder spoke out, with: '*honesty is the best policy Anna,*' and I thought okay, right, *don't lie to her*, but the devil convinced me…. "I don't know what you mean, Mum," I said quietly, waiting. And she looked back at me steadily and silently for a moment. Was she disappointed in me? I thought suddenly. She pursed her lips to continue just as an exuberant little voice broke in,

"She's madeing my t-shirt all cleaner, she's gonna do it 'cos it's been on two dirty days." Elsie smiled winningly up at Mum, who took a moment to refocus her gaze away from me and raising her eyebrow said sadly and gently, "Well she's a lovely big sister, and I know that she would do anything for you, cheeky chops, but don't keep asking her." She glanced at me holding my gaze a split second too long and continuing, "Sometimes Anna is a bit too kind for her own good, and maybe she needs to share the load a little bit."

She turned away slowly, her head on one side and I saw her falter. I held my breath, watching her, waiting, while Elsie cavorted around my legs pulling at my trousers breathlessly, performing an enthusiastic, uncoordinated dance, and Libby sat on the dining room floor, gazing at me steadfastly and silently, her piece of toast soggy and forgotten in her hand.

"Don't be so determined that the decision you just made was the right one, for me or for any of us darling," she said gently as she walked away, "this is a small house and you need us all."

The dust motes twirled in the wake of warm air left behind her, and for a moment I was frozen, shamed almost. It seemed as though even River Meadow Cottage was on tenterhooks, waiting for the next instalment of the strange, upsetting conversation. My hand reached down to check Elsie at the very moment Libby spoke. "Mummy sad," she said in a quavery voice, and she looked up at me her blue eyes unblinking, her lip wobbling. "I know, Libby," I said softly, bending and gently scooping her up, holding her close, "but it's ok, I'm going to give her a big cuddle and we're going to have some girl time." I looked at them both in turn, questioningly, "I think that's probably the decision I should have made after all, don't you?" They nodded seriously, one at a time and Elsie said, "I fink so cos Mummy lubs hugs and gwirl time."

God, I tried so hard to find a good time to speak to Mum. Oh, I had the opportunity a couple of times over the next day or two and maybe so did she, but I struggled with an opener, a prequel to the conversation that I knew was going to turn her world upside down. I didn't really consider that perhaps it was the same for her.

I fought with the knowledge that I was going to offload on her, the confusion, fear, and the worry that I felt whenever I allowed myself the time to think about *'things'*. And as it turned out in the end, the tête-à-tête happened accidentally, and afterwards, admittedly quite a long time afterwards, I was so thankful it had happened to at least demonstrate that it was after all, a *gift*.

"Elsie get your coat and shoes, we're going down the shop," Mum called chirpily, a few days later. "Come on, Libby, see if you can get ready first." The girls rushed to the hall and grabbing coats and shoes, hunkered down on the stone floor to win the very frequent and familiar competition of who could be coated and booted first. I bent down to do up Libby's buckles, she did struggle with them, her baby fingers still so clumsy, while Elsie was busy with the tip of her tongue poking out, face full of concentration, doing her own buckles, *'like a big gwirl'*.

"I need to put my purse in my basket this time," Mum said, "I can't be asking for credit again, it gets embarrassing." She pouted her lips in the hall mirror, and deftly ran her lipstick over them and shrugged into her coat picking up the errant purse.

We shooed the girls out of the front door and up the bumpy drive, playfully smacking their bottoms to chivvy them on as they giggled and squabbled in childish excitement. "Bye Daddy," they yelled as they hopped and skipped their way past the lawn where Dad was cutting the grass, his white sun hat perched skew whiff on his lightly perspiring head.

⊷⊷⊱⟨ ⟩⊰⊶⊶

Chapter 5 – 1976 – The Incident

"You are thirteen, darling, not thirty," Mum said tersely, with an attempt at a stern face. "You do *not* have to be the Mum to those two imps, you really don't," she continued on, gathering pace, getting into the swing of her 'little chat'.

"I'm the Mum, you are my child and you need to stop babying those girls, they ask too much of you, and *you* can't seem to say no!" She pointed at me irately, "At this rate you'll be an empty carcass, a husk by the time you're fourteen, just a shadow, worn out, with hands like a washer woman."

We both started to giggle at the ridiculous over dramatism of her words, and suddenly it seemed possible she'd forgotten what she wanted to talk to me about. Part of me was amused, the childish part, the part with nothing on my mind other than the indulgence of my little sisters; the other part well, that part was waiting rather tensely to see if, after all, she remembered what had prompted these diverting theatrics.

The girls were running ahead, busy jumping the fence pole shadows lining the field on the path at the top of Cottage, and picking the beginnings of the leggy cow parsley. Mum had presumably taken this opportunity, on our way to the shop on a Saturday morning when Dad was mowing the grass and Jon was on his paper round, to broach what was obviously an extremely tricky chat. I was at a bit of a loss to know how to even start that conversation.

It had to be me though I thought, I had to own it. I took a deep breath; "Mum ..." I started, looking ahead, focussing on anyone but her. She was silent, just a step behind me on the path, and I watched the girls caper happily, up ahead, and wondered if she was ignoring me on purpose.

I turned to stare at her in the pale spring sunshine and shivered as a cloud went over the sun much to Libby's disgust, she was well ahead in the shadow jumping game, and I was suddenly caught and transfixed by the look on Mum's face. She was squinting hard over my head, along the village road, her body tensed, exuding an almost feral fascination, her eyes narrowed, her limbs locked in a forward position, silent and poised, ready to strike. I saw her pupils narrow and pinpoint.

In a split second, anxiety flooding through me, I turned to follow her gaze but I couldn't see anything. I let out a long breath, nothing, the road was clear, the sky a beautiful halcyon blue, a fine spring day just like any other. But then suddenly, just as I started to breathe again, over the crest of the slightest of dips up ahead, a boy appeared, a young boy on a bike racing in our direction on the opposite side of the little village road, his head down, parker hood shielding most of his face, all except his wide smile, his legs pedalling like the wind in free and happy childish abandon. I smiled too at his exuberance and then in recognition; Jon, and then I saw, with sudden horror, what she must have seen.

With his head down and his hood up, he was going to ride at breakneck speed into the back of the parked coal lorry.

With my heart pounding out of my chest, in frantic haste, I started to raise my hands towards my ears, I could stop this. I knew I could, but before they were even half way there I was decelerated completely, my limbs heavy and immovable. I heard a distant murmur, felt a soft tremor in the air, a gentle wave of white noise. My vision distorted, blurred suddenly, and the world slowed to such a pace, became so still that it was almost like a photograph, taken in the palest of sepia tones.

I was numb, and so frightened, the world around me moved as though it were caught in some glutinous, watery liquid. It was like trying to see through tracing paper. Oh my God, *Jon*.

I watched helplessly through the distortion, in utter bowel loosening panic, as Mum strode over to Jon, who was frozen and immovable, still miraculously upright on his bike, feet on the pedals, his hood curtaining all but his smile, and she very gently lowered him, still on his bike, onto the grass verge of the road, where he clung to the handlebars smiling in an immobile parody of happy abandon.

"Oh no, Jon's taken a spill," I suddenly heard Mum speak beside me in a surprisingly strident voice, and she turned back towards the road, and walked over to help Jon up off the verge, where he was raising himself lazily, still grinning like a street urchin, only two, horrifically short feet away from the back of the parked coal lorry.

Snap.

My entire world jerked back into focus with vicious speed, leaving me reeling and lightheaded. I didn't seem to have any other choice though, I shook my head slowly, clearing the fog, dropping my still raised hands back to my sides, and I watched and tried to comprehend the incident. I was caught up in the absolute confusion and wonder, of the aftermath of one of the most intriguing and fascinating moments of my young life.

"Anna, mine's a gobstopper," Jon yelled cheekily to my dazed countenance, as he cycled round the tail of the lorry, back to River Meadow Cottage, for his breakfast.

"Mine is a stopgobbder too," Elsie wailed plaintively, while Libby sat on the path prising dried chewing gum off the pavement, just up ahead.

I felt disconnected, fragile, and afraid. I turned, "Mum …" I managed tearfully.

"Shhh," she said gently. "I know, shhh, everything's ok", she reached for my hand smiling. "This is a conversation I've been waiting to have with you, I think I could have timed it better, but darling, we can talk about this, about everything, just let's wait until we're alone, okay?"

Chapter 6 – 1976 – The Explanation

"We're going to bake, Samuel," Mum said firmly, "could you take the girls across to the river please, …and Jon", she added glancing appraisingly at my brother's already muddy knees and his air of suppressed and potentially volatile, mischief. Dad looked up spectacularly slowly and resignedly from the Sunday paper, which he had finally found hidden under the hall door mat. He was notorious on a Sunday morning for immersing himself so completely in the hallowed print that no one could breach his absorption, I had therefore gone to extraordinary means to try and combat the poor man's one moment of weekly peace so he could spend more time with us. He was the best fun, so off the wall, open to even the most complex and convoluted thought processes, which were turned over, discussed, dissected, and finally unity was reached through team agreement, even little Libby had a chance to voice her opinion.

Last night's discussion had been instigated by Elsie who had randomly asked why people get blind dogs. It turned out she thought the dog was blind rather than the owner, but having been informed that it was the owner that was blind and 'couldn't see', asked in absolute horror, *'how'd he get down the pub then?'* Mum had pointed out kindly, that maybe getting to the pub wasn't the most important drawback to being blind, but Dad had interposed, stating quietly but firmly, *"Don't be ridiculous Katarina, it's possibly one of the most imperative disadvantages to loss of sight,"* to which a lot of undignified sparring of words and giggling had ensued, ending finally with Libby saying that Dad always smelled when he came back from the pub, and Mum adding, coquettishly, that at least he smelt marginally better than a blind dog.

The crew, and a world-weary Dad, disappeared out of the front door to shouts of *"open the gate and stop swinging on it"* and *"Libby, up and over darling, you can't fit under there, now can you!"*

Mum turned towards the pantry saying over her shoulder, "We've probably got half an hour, let's bake and talk, shall we? I've got so much I want to say to you, and I've waited such a long time." Her blue eyes gleamed with suppressed excitement and love. I felt a moment of complete happiness wash over me. Time with Mum and a chance to talk. At last.

"When I was a child," Mum started, sifting the flour into the big old china bowl, with the hairline crack gracing its faded surface, "my Mum, your Gran, was said to have 'the gift'." She looked at me steadily, stirring the sugar into the mixture. I waited, I didn't ask, not yet. Mum added the butter to her own interpretation of a chocolate cake, and not one to be sniffed at, it was awe-inspiring, light, and airy and tasted better than anything bought from down the shop, or anything in fact, I'd ever had even.

"Her particular area of expertise," she continued, "was herbal medicine, oh she was marvellous." Mum smiled, remembering, "Everyone would come to her with all sorts of ailments; rashes and sores, headaches and sprains, palsy, chicken pox, oh so many different niggles. More even perhaps, than a doctor, nowadays, would get to hear about." She cracked the first egg into the bowl. "Back in those days, no one liked to bother the doctor, not when such a lovely, gentle, lady could help them perfectly well, someone right on their own doorstep, whom they trusted implicitly."

"You see," Mum said proudly, her eyes shining, "she never breathed a word, not to anyone, you couldn't prise her lips apart to tell a secret, even if you tried. She was a lady, a real lady. She treated everyone equally, big or small, rich or poor, they were all the same to her, just souls in distress who needed help, and oh she gave it so willingly, she gave everything she had to each of them." Mum gazed into the distance, her body still, the memories tripping through her mind.

Reaching out, she cracked the second egg into the mixture before turning to me. "She used the herbs, Anna, because she had no choice, you see, this is what I've wanted to talk to you about, but the time had to be right, to be perfect." She continued, wiping her floury hands off on her pinny. "The thing is darling; Gran didn't really need any herbs at all to help those people." She looked at me intently now, and enunciating slowly like she would to a small child she repeated, "She didn't actually need the herbs. Anna, do you understand?"

I looked back at her, caught in her stare, watching her eyes, letting myself fall into understanding, allowing acknowledgement of the silent message, the unsaid, the gift of trust just bestowed, from her, my Mother, to me. "Yes," I said suddenly, holding her gaze, …. "Yes, Mum, I do, I understand." My heart soared suddenly and a new understanding reached me. I wasn't alone, Mum and now Gran. My breath left my body, a stream of released tension flowing from me, so thorough I felt as though I might float off the face of the earth and vanish into space.

Her gaze unlocked from mine, and she smiled. She shone it seemed, from the inside out, and she turned slowly from me a little emotionally. Cracking the third egg into the bowl she said, looking down at the mixture, almost whispering, "In the end, you'll always get back, in one way or another, what you put in." The words were like a mantra … a chant.

I stood quietly beside Mum and together we prepared the rest of the cake mixture to put into the tins. I half wondered whether she would talk more to me, but we were both in a strange peace, a momentous minute of understanding, and I didn't feel the need to break the moment with her.

Voices reached us from outside, the babble of excitement, the low tones of Dad's laugh and Jon yelling, "Elsie, you need to stop throwing the spawn, those are little baby frogs, and you're hurting them," followed by a high-pitched voice wailing indignantly, *"I NOT frow baby frogs Jon I frow snot off my hand!"*

I turned to Mum quickly, a bit anxiously, I was worried I would lose the chance to tell her everything, to let her know what was really going on in my life, that maybe this moment would never come again. I said, "Can we do this again, Mum? I want to talk to you about something, something really important." She looked back at me calmly, smiling, and said, "Of course darling, there's a long way to go yet, and I know you want to talk to me, don't worry we're in this together, everything will be fine." She took my hand, "Together, okay? Listen darling, no more worrying, we are *all* in this together."

School on Monday took my mind back to more ordinary matters. I had loved school when I was attending in the village with Evie. Leaving there had changed so much for me. Mum and Dad hadn't liked the local secondary where most of my friends were going on to, even I had to admit to it being a bit rough and ready. But catching the bus with them, spending my days in familiar surroundings with Evie, and children I had known most of my life was persuasive. Nevertheless, something in me wanted more and I accepted that I wouldn't get it at the local secondary, even if it was soooo easy; only four miles away, host to all my allies, school bus, not public, picked up right outside the shop.

I started my new school, *twenty miles away*, by *bus*; *public*, one change, one half hour wait in between, it must be said, with a bit of an attitude, a slight resentment, and a bolshy, hard done by, *big mistake* feeling. I was right, I did hate it. I felt like, and even had dreams about, putting my fingers through the wire fencing around the tennis court and replaying my first day at 'big school', while crying to a passer-by to go and get my Mum.

Story of my life though, two miserable weeks after I started at the convent, brown uniform, 'brown' for God's sake! Two soulless weeks of sitting on buses for the hour and a half each way journeys, and along came Binny, my new and best friend, who changed my life for ever.

Caitlin Binnley, tall, willowy, black haired, laugh 'til you wet yourself, Binny. In build she was everything I wasn't, curvy while I was all skin and bone, tall where I was short, raven haired while I was blond, but our humour, well, it was like two twin souls meeting in a cascade of effervescent fireworks. Moreover, and joy of joys, she was a fellow sufferer, she lived even farther away from school than I did, and a mere six miles from me. The universe worked in mysterious ways indeed!

Chapter 7 – 1978 – The Party

"A party?" I'd squealed to Mum and Dad. "Really? Can Binny come?" It was early summer and the garden was looking lovely, so Mum and Dad thought a BBQ with a few people over would be fun. Fat Shaun from down the pub, Cad, the Elvis impersonator, weirdly, a tanned man with a beard, whom no one really knew, but was called Bris, short for Bristles, my Aunt Rose, a mere ten years older than me. A beautiful, gentle girl, and such a good laugh. Vinnie, so called because he put vinegar on all his veg, and Sneaky George, not invited but he'd turn up anyway. All those and a lot of word-of-mouth people were up for a night on the lawn, with what turned out to be: *isn't hindsight a proper enemy sometimes?* a BBQ cooked on an asbestos board, which Dad had unwittingly lined the base of the fire with.

"Binny," I hissed from the end of the dining room table where I crouched, "grab it quick, Mum will be back in five secs!" I'd made Binny purloin a bottle of Sweet Martini in a feat planned more thoroughly than the Great Train Robbery. We'd managed to open the drinks cupboard in the dining room, grab the Martini, and crawl in commando fashion, to the den outside River Meadow Cottage, namely an old caravan, still with working gas mantles, should there be gas, which unfortunately or even fortunately, there wasn't.

We were due to be sleeping there that night and the double bed at the back was made up for us to share. It was about as exciting as it could ever get for two fourteen-year-old convent girls in 1978.

"You first, take a glug to get us going and then me," I'd instructed. After all Binny had first dibs for being the main player, but I was in charge as it was my plan. We sat on the edge of the bed, our blankets neatly folded back, pillows artistically plumped. The old battery radio was tuned in and we had three cigarettes to share, half a Mars Bar, don't ask, as well as a loaf of Mother's Pride with a chunk of cheese for a midnight feast. We were set and it was turning out fabulously.

Or so we thought.

How could we possibly have guessed what the evening would lead to, and when we did know, we wished fervently we could undo everything, turn back the clock and make it all ok again, but even I couldn't change what happened, it was too dark and too big.

The sun had hardly set in the sky when the first inkling of unpleasantness began, and to start with it was just a small episode of rudeness, hardly noticeable to anyone else but a few of us, but it upset me and played on my mind.

I decided to keep watch, my mood apprehensive; there was something brewing and I couldn't think for the life of me why on such a glorious evening, with all our friends around us, there should be such a feeling of unwelcome expectation.

The walled lawn at River Meadow Cottage, was sheltered and edged with Michaelmas daisies, Forget Me Nots, Honeysuckle, Delphiniums and a host of wildflowers which Mum loved with a passion. In turn the garden seemed to give us its all, the chaotic mishmash of plants promoting a look of lush and happy, wanton abandon. It also exuded a wonderful scent, and in a gentle breeze the flowers swaying and rustling, it seemed like the garden was whispering endearments.

The BBQ next to the old garden wall, sent up its plume of grey smoke as the charcoal fought to stay lazy, sullen and unlit. The smell reminded me of holidays with the buzz of conversation and Jon telling his endless supply of jokes, somehow with a forbidden beer in his almost teenager hand, gesticulating and parodying the characters in his stories, while gusts of appreciative laughter met his words.

I watched as Binny lazily perused the edges of the lawn, half a head taller than some of the guests at nearly fifteen, her hair jet black against the vibrancy of the flowers; she was taking stock, this I knew, I wondered why she felt she needed to.

"You ok, Sis?" I jumped as Jon appeared beside me, his eyes now so much higher than mine, brown and enquiring. I was tense, I dropped my shoulders, rotating them to ease the stiffness. He looked at me questioningly, "What is it, what's up?" I decided to be honest with him, albeit just a little. "I don't know," I said slowly, looking him in the eye, "something feels wrong, Jon, out of place, oh I don't know." I huffed impatiently, "me being silly I bet, but I really don't want to feel like this, I want to enjoy the party." My glance darted around the lawn, trying to justify my feeling. "I just feel really worried for some irritating reason."

Jon turned away from me, and for a moment I thought he was going to throw me a platitude and then brush me off, but I saw that he was surveying the scene; the happy people all around us, Mum and Dad, close together smiling and chatting, Elsie and Libby scampering around with the kids from Island House right across the field, Fat Shaun standing by the BBQ waiting for first dibs no doubt; he'd have a long wait judging by how well the charcoal was holding out, Sneaky George by the drinks table, Bris … he paused and I turned my eyes to follow his gaze.

Binny her dark eyes impenetrable, also had her eyes locked on Bris from the other side of the lawn, as he made his way towards Aunt Rose, pausing just long enough to scoop up a bottle of beer from the garden table, his eyes never leaving her.

He stopped not far from her, his feet planted apart, tall and confident with his white shirt open and a leather thong necklace resting against the skin of his tanned chest. There was no doubt he was a good-looking man. He put his hand up to sweep his russet hair back and I caught a glimpse of an earring glinting in the evening light. As she lifted her head from taking a sip of her drink, he quickly turned his eyes away from her, gazing at the children cavorting around. I could see her gathering her courage in her hands, she was so shy, I also knew that I wanted to stop her from … from what though, was I being ridiculous? I hoped so, I wanted this to go well for her.

I started forward to join them, my steps falling in beside Jon as we walked across the trampled grass together, dodging the groups of cheery partygoers, and moving with purpose. It felt like we needed to somehow. Binny watched quietly from the side-lines, the last rays of the evening sun glinting on her raven hair.

We were almost upon them when Aunt Rose, smiling shyly, made her move. She turned to Bris, her face pink and animated and said daringly, "What's a nice boy like you doing in a place like this?" He turned to face her fully before replying slowly, both coldly and derisively, "Not speaking to you I hope, *my love*."

She jerked back, her face a picture of shock. Turning away quickly, she raised an unsteady glass to her lips, a flood of mortified colour rising on her cheeks. I was shocked by the meanness of Bris too, but I could actually feel Jon's annoyance, it came from him in waves, and as though he could sense it, Bris glanced towards him quickly, his face suddenly morphing into an affable smile.

Jon cut in before he could speak. "Bris," he said sternly, with all the assurance of an aged, black capped Judge, "you really aren't welcome here, old chap, please leave," and to emphasise his point Jon swept his hand back towards the drive in a *'let me show you the exit'* sort of way. A soft voice halted him for a moment. "Jon," Aunt Rose interrupted gently, "it's ok darling, no real harm done, I'm ok." I saw Jon look at her for a moment, assessing her, before he said protectively, and I loved him for it "No, Aunt Rose, Bris will be leaving, because we don't want him here."

"This way, Bris," Binny's voice, low and firm, came from behind me suddenly. She stood tall and imposing. Reaching forward and taking Bris by the arm, she drew him, none too gently, away from the group, his face showing a brief flash of fury before he transformed his expression to impassive. They walked towards the drive, Binny holding his arm, to all the other guests it must have looked as though they were friends, going to get a beer from the drinks table.

"Rose," Cad shouted suddenly, pushing his way through the melee, his stomach confined but straining frantically against the wide collared, white silk shirt, in the style of his idol, completely oblivious to any lingering tension. "Come and sing, gal, you've the voice of an angel and Elvis needs you," and winking at her salaciously he dragged her by the arm, ignoring her repeated weak refusals, prompting a small smile to unbend her stiff features and banish the sadness of the horrible moment before.

"Nicely done, Jon," I said reaching to hug him briefly, catching a slight whiff of beer and cigarettes on his breath. I shook my head sighing at him in exasperation and he smiled back at me, once again the cheeky nearly teenager, his chest just a tad more puffed out than before, but swiftly, with his face falling and as it turned out, some sort of insight, he said: "Don't celebrate too soon, Sis, I've got a feeling we haven't heard the last of Bris, there's more to him than meets the eye."

Chapter 8 – 1978 – The Devastation

Wincing Binny took another glug out of the dark bottle and turning to me said wheezily, "Phew, thank God it's nearly gone, I don't think I could take much more of that, it's disgusting!" She fake gagged as I giggled, reaching unsteadily for the Martini bottle, and missing. We both laughed hysterically, jamming our hands into our mouths, trying to muffle the sounds as we hunched together in a secluded hollow under the tall laurel bushes which ran the length of the lawn.

The music echoed around the garden to the side of us, the hum of chatter had grown into a cacophony of sound; with Mum singing along to Leo Sayer at the top of her slightly slurry voice, there was no real chance that anyone would hear us.

"Shall we smoke one of our fags?" I stage whispered, causing another round of giggles, and Binny to produce an explosive round of guttural hiccups, which had us in more fits of eye watering, juvenile laughter. "Yessss," she whispered back eyes shining, "have you got the matches?" I delved around in my trouser pockets, and drew out a flattened box of Swan Vestas. "Yep, here, let's have one and lie back and relax."

The match flared and I shielded the flame with my hand and lit up the cigarette like a professional. The sharp smell of sulphur mixed with the simple scent of the laurels, the damp earth and trampled grass added to the moment. Binny and I had practised inhaling and to our surprise, we quite liked it. It had taken a bit of perseverance, but never ones to give up, we worked through the problem areas together, i.e., choking, coughing and nausea.

"Moments like this don't come around very often, Binny," I said with Martini induced authority as I exhaled the smoke luxuriously, passing the glowing cigarette to Binny, "and we're going to make the very most of them." Her eyes gleamed back at me in the darkness, and the glint of her teeth and a small, hastily subdued cough, told me she was smiling in full agreement.

I don't know when the noise changed, when the music became less melodious, less harmonious. A feeling of unease hit me hard though, and bought me down from the earlier simple contentment with a rush. I felt the hairs on the back of my arms rise and an involuntary shudder shook my whole body. "Binny?" I whispered uneasily into the darkness. "Yes, I know," she answered slowly, "I feel it, let's check it out." We eased the leafy branches apart carefully and gazed out onto the lawn.

The moon in its imperturbable glory, rode high in the sky, outlining the thatch of River Meadow Cottage in a cool silver light, the chimney pots like 3D cut outs. The curtains were drawn in the girls' room upstairs, they'd been put to bed earlier in the evening, with the inevitable arguments from Elsie about how "it's not fair, I'm not tired, I'm a big gwirl" while rubbing her eyes and being too exhausted to put her arm through her nightie sleeve. Libby just slept like a log as she was hoisted into the bottom bunk, her pigtails still in their Peter Rabbit bows.

The lawn looked eery and mystical, an image of looking into a snow globe came to mind, it was both magical and dreamlike, yet somehow impossible. A low mist had settled around the legs of the guests, where the heat of the lawn met the chill of the night air. Binny and I were transfixed, momentarily robbed of our speech. We were shoulder to shoulder kneeling on the damp earth, peering out from the sanctuary of our leafy den, unable to tear our eyes away. I was glad of the warmth of Binny's arm pressed close to mine; it was the most unnerving sight.

Our friends still stood in their groups, but the lively conversation had gently ebbed, fading away as though some kindred understanding had woven its way through them all, leaving behind a universal, silent agreement. Yet still the strident music mocked the mood, it's shrill tones almost derisive against the ethereal cottage garden. It was a jumble of inexpert comparisons, a mishmash of inappropriate contrasts. It was discordant and unpleasant, but why was it, what was wrong?

My eyes searched the guests, Cad, Aunt Rose, Mum and Dad, standing but weaving slightly, Sneaky George hogging the last garden chair, Walt and Prid from Island House, Fat Shaun, Vinnie, holding a cold hot dog, no doubt covered in vinegar, the late comers, who turned up half cut after closing time, even Old Tommy, the gardener, ancient and wizened, sitting next to Mr Gilbert, I knew them all; I had done for years. Still, we watched, unable to think what needed fixing, or how to fix it. From the stillness a movement in the centre of the lawn caught my eye.

Bris.

He walked towards Mum slowly, his face emotionless, arms hanging by his sides. The groups followed his progress with their collective eyes. She gazed back at him impassively, her breathing even, but knowing her like I did, I could see the unease, the way she held her arms, her head. Dad without moving from her side, seemed to close the space between him and Bris, his stance broadening, his expression hardening, a look I barely recognised washing across his face.

Bris continued on, narrowing his eyes, and stopping just a few feet from them. He made a slight almost imperceptible, upwards jerk of his head towards Mum, who suddenly flew backwards, landing heavily on her side in the Michaelmas Daisies, her limbs an untidy tangle.

I gasped out loud, my hand flying to my mouth as I launched myself out of the laurels, at the same time as Dad leapt towards Bris, his hand grabbing Bris' throat with unerring accuracy, and lifting him high from the ground, roared into his face, spittle coating his lips, "Go home, Bris, before I forget I am a decent human being. Do not challenge us again, you cannot hope to win."

He let Bris drop to the ground, gasping, his good-looking face now blotchy and unattractive, and turning to Mum, Dad offered his hand, "Up you get darling, are you a bit squiffy?" He smiled down at her and gazing into his eyes she took a moment and said decisively, "I think I am, Samuel. What am I like?" Reaching down, Dad stroked her cheek lovingly. "Perfect is what you are my love, just perfect."

Without turning, Dad said over his shoulder, "Anna darling, it's …. headache time … after all that …. Martini," he glanced around at the silent guests who stood waiting, mouths agape, for the next interesting instalment.

I gawked back at him, aghast, almost undone at the extent of his knowledge, and he turned and nodded at me gently before adding quietly, "Please." I guessed I would be taking us back, taking us to the moment before Bris made it back onto the lawn, before Mum *'fell drunkenly'* into the daisies.

But I was too late, it was all too late.

As I turned, raising my hands to my head, Bris launched himself up from the ground, swift and sure, his face purple with rage, his frustration and fury boiling over; and lunging at Jon, he grabbed him savagely around the neck, and twisted with all his strength.

Jon didn't even have a chance to register the pain, the resounding, single crack of bone left us screaming in anguish, as Jon's young body fell to the ground in a broken, lifeless heap. His eyes, still and lifeless, gazed across the lawn onto an unknown horizon.

I heard the screaming around me, and saw the chaos as though the world were in slow motion. The guests caught in the dreadful, cataclysmic moment, the unearthly cries that came from my Mother's lips, on and on, echoing across the misty grass, and the torture on my Father's face etched into my mind. The world swam before me, and a pain of loss like I had never known before surged through me, drowning me with its intensity.

Through it all I heard a voice, Aunt Rose, gentle and insistent, over and over again,

"Take us back Anna, take us back, Anna, take us back, quickly darling, quickly, Anna take us back! … now darling, do it NOW!" her voice vibrated through my head, like a woodpecker, relentless, persistent, and dully I raised heavy, bloodless, hands to my head. I didn't know how to make this work; I didn't know if I was strong enough. What if I couldn't?

I had never done anything like this before nothing as big, nothing, *God damn it,* I was messing with death.

My breath came unsteadily. I couldn't save him; all I could do was clean a dirty t-shirt. A million doubts swamped me even though all the time I kept on raising my hands through the glutenous air, to catch hold of my ears. I was too afraid, I couldn't do it, I hesitated; and a strong urgent voice spoke firmly over my shoulder.

"Yes, you can Anna, you can do this, I'll help you, come on, *now*, *right now*, come on, there's not much time." Binny was standing behind me, the bond of our friendship reaching me through the chaos, and placing trembling arms around my neck, her cheek resting on the top of my head, said frantically, "We'll do it together. *Do it, God Anna,* do it now!"

A rage like I had never known before hit me hard in the chest, almost causing me to faint with its power. Blood pounded through my head, my fingers and toes pulsed with fury, the rage burning me up, and Binny, I knew, felt it rise too, a brutal heat flowing from my body, its intensity rising like bile into my throat, rancid and sour. "Use it," Binny said urgently. "Use it Anna, save him."

Chapter 9 – 1978 – The Morning After

I woke to bright sunshine beating through the curtains upstairs in River Meadow Cottage, a slight summer breeze gently stirring the edges of the material. The girls' bunk beds lay empty across from me, neatly made, the ironed sheets folded back tightly over the blankets, hospital corners sharp against the battered pine.

Low sounds came from the garden outside, and I could faintly hear Elsie and Libby chatting quietly together. I smiled slightly, something was amiss, those two were never quiet. Why were the beds made?

My neck was stiff, I could feel it. I turned my head slowly, flinching; discomfort raced across my forehead, radiating lower into my ears in a heavy throb of hot agony. Groaning out loud in shock and pain, I screwed my eyes up in a tight wince, hardly daring to breathe. What. The. Hell? Why was I feeling like I'd gone ten rounds with Cassius Clay, what had happened? I tried sifting through my memories for a clue, but I couldn't seem to pierce the dense fog, I couldn't think what the year was, let alone the day. What was going on?

"Mum," I cried out in a panic, "Muuuum". A moment of silence followed and then the latch on the stair door rattled erratically and a heavy pounding on the stairs, gradually presented a flood of people that had me take a couple of painful breaths in surprise.

Mum and Dad jammed themselves in the bedroom door, both trying to get through at the same time, followed by Binny, peering over their shoulders, her eyes wide and shadowed, and I could hear Elsie through the window shouting at Libby in the garden, "She's awake, she's awake, come on." Their little footsteps clattered on the path and then the steps outside as they rushed in through the dining room to the bottom of the stairs, their little voices squabbling, "Me first, me, no me, it's my turn," and a humph of childish annoyance and a wailed, "It's not fair, you done it last time," from the loser, bringing a weak smile to my aching face.

"You're awake, Anna." Mum elbowed her way past Dad, and rushing to my bed, sank to the floor beside the bed in one fluid movement. Looking deep into my eyes, she brushed my hair back tenderly. "How are you feeling darling?" Her voice was husky and unsteady. I looked at her searchingly and then past her at the waiting crowd.

"I think I'm ok, I have a really bad headache, though." I said questioningly, "What happened?" and before she could open her mouth to reply, it all came crashing back in an instant, and a heavy, sudden and horrific awareness hit me:

"Jon …..." my voice rose frantically in a piercing scream, "where is he, oh my God, where's Jon? Jonnnnnn……"

A wail of utter anguish came out of my mouth, I couldn't believe such an inhuman noise had left my body; it was a mere second, but felt like a lifetime. Mum kneeling beside me mouthing words I couldn't hear, Dad rushing towards me, arms outstretched, trying to calm me, before a soothing and comforting voice, the only voice I wanted to hear, and thought I never would again, filtered determinedly through my jagged breaths, making me stop and strain my ears to check I wasn't mistaken.

"I'm right here, Sis, I'm here Sis, it's all ok, stop now," and he forced his way past them, pushing them out of his path without a care. He was wearing his old pyjamas, three inches too short, his hair all mussed, but I could see he stood tall and strong. I could see his brown eyes. I couldn't take my eyes off his face, and I watched him say stuff I couldn't decipher, his lips moved but no sound reached my ears; the terror overrode everything, I just couldn't believe he was alive.

Taking a seat on the edge of the bed he reached for my shaking hands, clasping them both firmly, allowing me to recognise in the strength of his grip and the warmth of his skin, to acknowledge that this was real, not a dream, and he really was ok. Bruised, shaken, but ok.

Hours passed in the bedroom; the sun had started to go down before I could start to make some sort of sense of what had happened to us all on the evening of the party.

Mum and Dad went downstairs to make a picnic to bring up, the girls were ecstatic and had Mum's best green blanket on the floor in the middle of the room. A jug of orange juice with bits of fruit floating in it graced the centre of the rug, just begging for Elsie or Libby to knock it over, and they both sat staring at me with big eyes, wanting to come and sit on the bed, but under strict instructions not to be too overexcited and wear me out.

"Come on then," I said to them, smiling, and they hurled themselves onto the bed, the juice jug wobbling precariously and just righting itself, as they rushed past, cuddling into me, my arms around them. I could smell the sunshine on them, and shampoo alongside an unusual smell of soil, but I didn't ask. They nuzzled in and reaching up, Libby gently ran her fingers over my hair, pausing here and there to say in a singsong voice, "ahhhh, it's ok, sooooon be better," before running her fingers gently over my eyes and crooning, "No more tears now, everythink is ok." Her little body rocked back and forth comforting me like a baby. Elsie sucked her thumb slurpily and rested against me, her warmth heavy on my chest, saying in a muffled voice, "We was sad, you wouldn't wake up."

I raised confused eyes to Binny and Jon, and simultaneously they mouthed "later" silently shaking their heads in unison.

Chapter 10 – 1978 – The Discussion

Later that night, the girls went to bed in Mum and Dad's room so that we could talk. River Meadow Cottage only had two bedrooms, but the landing was big enough to hold a single bed for Jon, and the girls and I slept in one room, and Mum and Dad had the other. It was very cosy, but we had never known a different way, and if we had, we still wouldn't have swapped.

Once the girls were bathed and fast asleep, Dad shut the bedroom door and Binny and Jon and Mum and Dad all squashed together onto my bed and the bottom bunk. They would have sat on the green rug, but the orange juice jug had left the most giant wet patch when it eventually went over, and Mum was still picking bits of fruit out of the wool.

I was caught between wanting to know absolutely everything, and being too scared to find out what had happened, and secondly, I was worried what damage had been done by the act I had performed. What on earth had the party goers made of the events of last night?

After Libby had stroked my head, the throbbing headache had nearly gone and I was actually feeling more human. I had a couple of sore patches above my ears. I think I must have pulled at my hair when I was reaching up for the 'headache' and I was wracking my brains trying to imagine how the rest of the evening had played out, how they had put things right, why people weren't knocking at the door, asking questions that we couldn't answer.

"Ok," said Dad "we are going to fill you in on the bits you don't know Anna." He looked at Binny and Jon gravely,

"It's probably best if you save the questions until the end, is that ok?" Both of them nodded seriously and I knew that they would both respect his wishes entirely, no matter what.

"Bris was not invited to the party," he said sighing heavily. He looked down at his hands and Mum reached out to stroke his arm encouragingly. He looked up at her questioningly, and she nodded back at him. "He really isn't our sort of chap at all," he continued, "he's a bit of a bad egg really, and we felt that, well, we have always known that he wouldn't fit in with our family." He paused and Mum said quietly, "Samuel, darling, this is going to take ages, shall I do it?"

He nodded at her thankfully and she turned to us.

"Right, Binny, Jon, here we go," she took a huge breath and practically blurted out the words. "Right well, let's see, um … well as you saw, Anna has an … unusual skill, and last night, well unfortunately, she had to use her skill to ensure Jon's, um … safety." She paused searching for the words, her hands still in her lap, while Dad looked at her apprehensively. She continued, "Anna has to the best of my knowledge, never used her skill in a situation such as the one we were faced with last night."

Jon and Binny were both silent and continued to look at Mum, waiting for her next words, their expressions blank. Even the air was still, waiting for the explanation that would make everything understandable, the unreal, real, the inexplicable, suddenly explicable.

"Look," she said, "I can beat around the bush all night, trying to make this seem normal, but you obviously know that it isn't. It isn't normal and what happened last night was an incredible, unbelievable, and wonderful reprieve for this family." "It was an act of love," she looked at me affirming her words and continued, "from Anna to her brother." Jon glanced across at me, almost speaking, reaching for my hand, when Dad cut him off gruffly, "Not yet Jon, let Mum go on."

"Now the thing is, when an act such as the one Anna performed on the night of the party takes place," she continued, "then it becomes tangible, it upsets the balance, let's just say it alters the stability of our future, it affects the settings you see, and very importantly, it could open us to harm." She looked at me carefully, "It means that we could now be in a precarious position, and we need to ensure, going forward, that we are protected." "Katarina," Dad said warningly. "Yes I know, Samuel," she said impatiently, "but better they are scared than dea.." her voice broke a little, but she visibly pulled herself together, and continued firmly and looking round at us one by one said, "better you are scared than dead."

We all remained silent, our faces trained on them, our bodies immobile, locked in an impasse, still waiting for the impossibly plausible explanation of the night before.

"Can I speak?" I said hesitantly into the silence, while Mum and Dad stared at each other, locked in a moment the rest of us did not understand. "Yes, you can, darling, out of all of us, you have that right," Mum replied quietly.

"Where is Bris?" I asked.

The eye lock moment, between them became more tense, and Dad dragged his eyes away to look at me. "He left the party," he replied briefly. "We don't know where he is, as yet," he paused and took a moment. "Anna, we do need to tell you what happened after, well after your headache, it's important you know what transpired, and how the party ended, all the other questions can be answered afterwards, and," he said looking at Jon affectionately, "Jon also needs to know what happened, even if it is deeply unpleasant for all of us. Everyone needs to be in the loop. We will of course explain everything we can. Now Binny," he continued, "you have been dragged into the most appalling and desperate situation, it is my absolute belief that you should have the choice to be removed from these circumstances."

He glanced at her and continued, "However, we have a problem. Now that we are …. um… traceable, for the moment you are stuck with us, none of us can perform any act to ensure your safety." He sighed heavily, "I'm so sorry darling girl, you are trapped with us for the time being, can we rely on your discretion? Your silence is imperative to our safety." We all turned our gazes towards Binny, our faces casting shadows on the bedroom wall behind us.

Lifting her chin, and squaring her shoulders she answered quickly, "I wouldn't want to be anywhere else Mr James, you can rely on my silence and support, for as long as necessary." Dad looked at her fondly, and the rest of us turned to her, smiling our thanks and approval. Her blush deepened when Jon reached out his hand and patted her on the shoulder, saying, "Well done, Binny."

"Dad," I said hesitantly into the brief moment of warmth, "you said none of us could perform any act right now? What did you mean exactly?"

Dad screwed up his eyes, in a giant flinch, and Mum looked at him in exasperation. "You'd better tell them, hadn't you, darling?" she said impatiently. "Go on then for goodness' sake."

Dad had obviously recognised the benefit of getting to the point less pedantically, and based on Mum's strident example, he forged ahead, leaving us open mouthed with his no-frills revelations, and that included Mum, who looked at him like he had suddenly developed two heads.

"Both your Mother and I have a skill each," he said briskly, "a skill that was born to us through generations of Romanies in Mum's case and in mine, well I'm not entirely sure, but suffice to say both my parents – Gran & Pops were …. alternative, um … new age travellers. Of course, we lived in a double decker London bus." Like that explained everything...

I looked across at Jon, but he was honed, with eyes like saucers on Dad, who gazed into the distance, obviously searching for ways to make this a child friendly explanation. Dad was so protective, he wanted nothing to prevent our childhood being perfect, he was such an idealist. But I saw him shake his head briefly, sadly too, and suddenly knew he couldn't do it. It was going to be hardcore, much as he wanted it to be different. I swallowed nervously.

"Now, your Mother has the ability to perceive future events, particularly events that may endanger her, or our loved ones, she has the ability to, to slow down time to prevent disaster, to allow for defensive action to be taken. Mum is what is known as a Foreseer." He paused for breath, glancing at her, his face unreadable, before continuing, "Unfortunately due to the um, party um, atmosphere, and Bris having already left the party, we were unable to foresee the events that took place last night." Mum closed her eyes in pain, I knew she was thinking back to how many drinks she had necked, and he took her hand before continuing.

"I," he said slowly, while the rest of us looked at him vacuously, "am not entirely sure what my particular skill is, it is possible that, that I am a Charmer." That admission brought Mum out of her moment of distress, and she sucked her breath in sharply. "Samuel," she blurted out looking at him incredulously. Holding up his hand to stop her, he said firmly, "Katarina, it's what I've been thinking for a long time, let's just keep calm darling, sometimes you have to face things head on, we can't just keep on pretending it isn't what it is." "Well, I never," she huffed hotly and indignantly, "well really!"

"Mr James?" a thin questioning voice rose from the bottom bunk. "Could I just ask, would you mind explaining something please?" Dad looked over at a shaky Binny and nodding sympathetically at her said, "Of course, Binny, please do."

I noticed for the first time how tired she looked, her eyes were dark in her pale face and her raven hair was unbrushed and lifeless. My poor Binny, she'd been dragged into this nightmare and now she was trapped, without even her Mum or Dad to talk to. Not that she would talk to her Mum, they were poles apart; Binny tall and willowy with her dark eyes and hair, wild at heart, burning for adventure, full of mischief, and her Mum, so very different; small and petite with mousey hair and so very many practical ideals, mostly tied up with housekeeping, oh and the something else, that Binny would never discuss. I could practically hear her sniffing her disapproval and disappointment at her wayward daughter. There was no chance of a sit-down chat about this, oh no, not with her, there was no safe harbour there.

But her Dad, I smiled just at the thought of him, now there was a man she could turn to. He was such a love, tall like her, with a cracking sense of humour and she was the apple of his eye. She adored him right back of course, but how to explain this to him? She couldn't, could she, how would that conversation go? She'd never be able to see me again. What parent in their right mind would want her mixed up in whatever this was? She was on her own with this, and my heart broke for her.

As though he could read me, Jon looked straight at me for a second, and turning he took Binny's limp hand in his, "It's ok, Binny, you're a part of this family now, we'll keep you safe, it'll all work out, you'll see." He waited for her to gather herself together, and she straightened her spine, and squeezing his hand back for a brief moment murmured quickly, "Here goes then," before turning quickly to Dad.

"Look, about Bris, Mr James, I've got to ask, why? What happened? Did he really throw Mrs James backwards into the daisies? Why was he so angry? I'm sorry but this all seems a bit heavy, a bit dramatic over a little spat in the garden!" She paused for breath and turning to me said tiredly, "I don't get it, Anna, oh I get some stuff," and she looked at me meaningfully. I had never explained about my headaches, but she had always just seemed to accept me, quirks and all, and we had left it like that, no questions asked.

"But ...", she continued, "what is this really about? It seems to me, that there's a whole lot going on here that we," and she took in me and Jon in her look, "don't have any idea about. I think, without being rude, Mr and Mrs James," she looked apologetically at them both, "that you need to tell us everything, from the beginning, because this, well this jumble of facts, well it's not good enough, really sorry, but it isn't."

She let out a big breath as Jon stared at her with his eyebrows raised in silent admiration, while a sense of relief that someone else but me had demanded the truth, washed over me; I really wasn't up to doing it myself, God I was tired. I looked at her gratefully and she fluttered one tired, dark, eyelid back at me in our trade mark secret code for thumbs up.

"Ok," Dad said. They looked at each other nodding silently, "We'll start at the beginning …"

Chapter 11 – 1951 – Rina

The vardos stood in a circle, each pair pointing to the other, doors open to the dusk air, their painted wheels gleaming in the last of the light. Sweet scented apple smoke rose lazily from the heart fire, its perimeter surrounded by granite stones, unbroken in size with old, virtually indistinguishable symbols carved into their ancient surfaces. A huge blackened kettle hung low on its tripod frame, simmering gently above the fire, singing its secrets to the glowing red embers beneath, while the horses snickered at their tethers, tugging grass from its roots and chomping noisily as they relaxed after the heat of the day.

As the wind sighed through the camp, rustling the lace hanging at the windows of the wagons and stirring the ash to rise in eddies around the burning wood, distant voices carried across the glen in the evening air and a young girl's voice rose in childish delight,

"I've found some Mam, look, look here!" There was a slight pause before another voice spoke, "So you have, my babe." Her Mother's voice, gentle with the inflection of old country spoke warmly but quickly. "Go on pick it quick, take it to Gram as fast as you can, she'll get it ready, the kettle's singin' even now."

Hurried footsteps rushing through the trees surrounding the river, brought the girl racing into the camp clutching a small sprig of white flowers in her hands, her face alight with pride. "I've got some, Gram, I found it, Mum didn't, *I did*." She paused for breath, her voice faltering, as she took in her

Gram, sitting on her stool outside the van facing theirs, her shawls wrapped tightly around her shoulders, her long skirts brushing the dry earth. Lost in her thoughts.

The girl watched her Grams trembling, blue veined hand stirring her cup, over and over again, then tipping the liquid into the saucer to gaze avidly back into the remaining leaves, her lips quivering violently as she mouthed what sounded like murmured, agitated chants, her head shaking in time to some desperate beat. "Gram …?" she said unsteadily.

She watched helpless, the flowers still clutched in her hand, as Mam hurried past her, reaching out to Gram, running her hand down her face softly calling to her, crooning an old song, that Rina hadn't heard before, then when the old lady had looked up, still confused and lost, frightened, her lips trembling, Mam led her slowly up the steps and into her van, her old boots mounting the worn steps with weary hopelessness, and she shut the door firmly behind them.

The Others gathered around the fire, their watchful eyes gentle with knowledge and sadness, taking the girl into their arms, comforting her, and talking of times past, stories designed to make her relax and forget her worries. The men smoked their clay pipes with stained teeth, gazing into the fire whilst the women stirred the pot adding herbs and spices, and broke the bread, handing out tin plates and cups with a swish of their skirts and a world of experience in their dark eyes.

The Watcher sat on the steps of his van, his eyes peering past the Romanies out into the darkness, his ears straining to hear anything amiss, his dog at his side, occasionally getting up to check the horses, running his hands down their legs to feel their heat, and holding out his rough hand to their soft lips, with slivers of apple, cut with his curved knife.

It was when a lull hit the subdued conversation that an eery sound was heard. It rose like the screech of a night owl, stretching itself out into a high, thin cry before starting over again. The cry was filled with melancholy; just listening to it drew a shiver from the others. As one they sprang to their feet and turned toward Gram's van, hands on knives, Mothers reaching for their children to draw them tight against their skirts.

Rina held her breath, her heart thudding almost out of her chest. She was frightened because she knew, without really knowing, that the meadowsweet would not have helped, nothing would have, those desperate chants, her Gram's red rimmed, defeated eyes told a different story.

Lylie found her just moments after the last unearthly cry had ceased. She strode down the steps of Gram's van, looking straight into Rina's eyes as though she knew exactly where she would find her. Striding across the camp she wrenched her roughly into her shaking arms holding her tight against the wool of her shawl, and while the tears ran unchecked down her pale cheeks and dripped onto the top of Rina's head, she keened her sorrow, her gentle voice hoarse and broken.

Rina's sobs rang out across the camp, and vaguely, like a dream, she could hear the others raising their voices in cries of loss alongside her and Mam, their moans of grief reverberating around the glen, as the roosting crows wheeled erratically out of the trees cawing their sadness.

Gram had gone, the mainstay in her world, her special friend, her ally, her mentor, her Matriarch, how could life ever be the same again? Clawing at her Mam's skirts she screamed out her pain as Mam held her close, letting the loss escape her small body. Her world seemed to swing on its axis, and flooded with her grief she couldn't accept, how could this be?

Rina was startled from a dreadful grey slumber the next morning with the sound of her Mam's voice as she leapt from the bench inside Gram's van, in the curious way she had of knowing when her husband was on his way home. Her eyes were red rimmed and broken, the sparkle gone and Rina wondered when, or if ever, it would return.

The two of them had sat together during the night, speaking to Gram, talking of memories and special moments, making sure she was never alone on the first stages of her journey. They held tightly to her cold hands, exuding their love for her into their grips, stroking her hair and gently smoothing away the dried tear stains from her cheeks. The intensity of their grief sat in their bellies like mounds of jagged, molten rock, eating at the core of them.

Lylie raced down the van steps, her feet bare and her hair flying behind her as the early sunlight picked out a distant shadow across the river meadow. "Tommy," she cried, "Oh Tommy." He strode into the clearing dropping his pack at his feet as he pulled her into his arms crushing her against him, his head lowered to her face as he cried unashamedly with her at the loss of her Mother. "I know darlin', she called to me, I felt her leaving, Lylie, and the birds went wild. I walked all night, I'm here, I've got you now, I'm here."

She sagged against him as other van doors opened and subdued calls of "Alright Tommy," "Glad's you'm back Tommo," echoed across the clearing. The children stood silently as he raised his head nodding to the others, and putting his arm around Lylie, he led her gently back to Gram's van.

Rina waited until he was inside before flinging herself at him and wrapping her arms tightly around his waist. He looked down at her sadly and brushing her hair back off her face held her tightly against him, looking down into her eyes, said softly, "You're gonna need to help your Mam, maid, this is hard on her, losing her own Mam." He set her down on the bench, and turning he fell to his knees beside the body of his Mother-in-law, the only real Mother he had ever had.

He'd loved her as his own and had rejoiced in the pride she took in him. "My Tommy this, my Tommy that" they roasted her rotten over how she could see him through rose tinted glasses. There was never a moment he had felt anything less than perfect in her eyes; they'd laughed together over their milk punches many a night, she'd been as sharp as he himself, and God knows he was sharp.

Gently smoothing her hair, his face lined with grief, he said quietly, almost hesitantly, "Something's not right though, Lylie, I felt it when she left, she cried out something to me, but I couldn't catch the stream, I reached for it, but it was too far away from me."

He compressed his lips in sorrow, trying to keep his emotions in check, "She called but I couldn't reach her in time." His voice broke as he strove to keep strong, and turning his head with her hand and looking deep into his eyes Lylie reached for him, wrapping him in her arms they keened their grief while the others outside joined their hands in pain at the sound, and raised their voices in harmony until the clearing was flooded by the sound of the Romany family joined in loss.

Rina wandered listlessly through the desolate camp later in the morning, the heart fire low in the stones, the grass trampled and flat, she could taste the sadness in the air and feel the heaviness of desolation steeped into the very ground. The rooks looked on, their black eyes shuttered, their voices silent.

All the vans had their doors and shutters closed in mourning, out of respect for their treasured Matriarch. Rina's heart felt heavy in her chest and touching the empty stool where Gram had sat only yesterday, made the pain in her belly shift like a leaden weight, grief rising hot and sour and almost choking her. She stroked the cushion softly, over and over, while she sobbed out heavy salty tears which felt like they would never stop, her heart hurt and she knew with certainty that she would never get over this loss.

Looking down she could see Gram's cup, the rose patterned china set down on the ground between the van and the chair, tucked up beside the wheel. Sobs hitching, she knelt and picked it up slowly, cupping it between her hands, holding on to it as though it were the most precious thing she had ever seen.

The china was beautiful, so fine it was almost translucent, Gram only had one cup and saucer. It had belonged to her Púridaia, her beloved Grandmother, and in her honour, she never used any of the tin mugs, she always tipped, *used to tip*, her breath hitched in her throat, the milky tea into the saucer to drink, so she could read the leaves.

Rina held the cup hardly daring to believe that she might be able to see what Gram had seen in the last moments of this life. What had she seen that had caused her to be so worried? It was almost too frightening to look.

"Rina?" came an anxious questioning voice from her Mother, coming down the steps of the van, "that's Mam's cup isn't it? Dear Lord, bring it here to me my babe." Sinking to her knees Mam sat heavily on the van step, her face twisted with grief. She took the cup and saucer with trembling hands, holding it like a precious artifact; "Come on my Rina, let's look together, there's no secrets between us. Tommy come out," she called, "Rina's got Mam's cup."

Van doors started to open and subdued voices drifted across the glen, then seeing the cup in Lylie's hands, they waited soundlessly. The Watcher paused too, his hooded eyes unreadable, as he stroked his dog's head and ran his thumb across the blade of his hunting knife. Huddled on the steps Rina and her parents looked at each other silently, before finally focussing their unwilling gazes onto the leaves.

Only a moment passed before Lylie drew in a sharp breath, her knuckles whitening on the delicate handle. Tommy raised his head slowly, gazing sightlessly into the trees at the edge of the river a vein pulsing erratically in his neck.

Slowly, Rina looked down, her fear almost driving her to run from the moment, but she couldn't, her need to know was absolutely overpowering. Mam looked at her, almost stopping her from continuing. Quickly she wrapped her small damp hands around the cup on top of her Mam's white knuckles, she focussed her eyes on the leaves; for a moment they swam with her tears before clearing and then, even to her young and inexperienced eyes, she understood with deep clarity what Gram had seen in the last moments of this life.

Chapter 12 – The Present – Lorentree Cottage

I took a deep breath, there was silence in Lorentree Cottage, apart from the logs crackling and the clock forcing its determined structure into the cosy room. The fire light danced on the walls and the coffee table sat with its half decimated, tasty load. Waiting. Watching.

I found myself with my head on the back of the arm chair, almost resting, the tension had ebbed from my shoulders and apart from some tingling in my feet, where I'd been sitting on them for so long, I was totally relaxed. How weird, that this, I mused languidly, the moment I had been dreading for most of my life was upon me, and I was saturated in a calm liquidity, which lapped at my limbs in easy, sanguine waves.

I lifted my head to a gentle touch and found Libby squatting beside the armchair stroking my hand while Elsie jumped up hurriedly, grabbing the wine, turning to fill glasses, her impatient nature fighting with her need to be considerate to me. No one spoke and I sat for a moment in the torturous silence, just waiting, but not knowing what I was waiting for. What now?

"Ahem" – a harmonious voice issued into the silence and as one, we all turned to face Jon expectantly, anxiously, all awaiting our brother's words. Slowly he turned to Elle, his waistcoat buttons sending out arcs of light, glancing off the walls like some strange hieroglyph, and in a leisurely fashion, raising his eyebrow and then his glass, he said with a roguish wink, "Mine's a Rioja please, Elsie."

We laughed long and hard, until the tears came, and then they really did come, even Jon wiped his eye surreptitiously, and I suddenly realised the depth of my sadness when I saw how different it all might have been, but *now* was my moment I thought resolutely, as the hope, the reality, blossomed across my chest, the warmth pooled in my stomach, here it was, the opportunity to share with people I loved and trusted. Now what sort of fool would I be, to turn down a chance like that?

I felt myself smiling, wider and wider, my face cracking, like some deranged Gypsy Rose, and they stared back at me, waiting, their faces unreadable, my loyal, patient sentinels, saying absolutely nothing.

"Get comfy, then," I said firmly, steadying my voice, and wiping my face free from the last vestige of tears, "this bit gets interesting."

Chapter 13 – 1951 – The New Matriarch

They were only keeping the cup and saucer, and the mystic ball. Mam said she would take them to Gram's graveside when she visited each day and Rina knew they would be here for a good year making sure Gram reached her new life safely. Her wedding ring and Pendant would be buried with her and of course her vardo would be burnt, it was tradition.

It hurt, all of it hurt but aside from her loss Rina could not reconcile to one inexplicable thing – the Pendant.

Of the few things Gram had owned, the Pendant called to her the most. Not for herself, of that she was sure, and in life hanging around Gram's neck she had hardly noticed it. But she did now. As it sat on Gram's unmoving chest nestled in the cotton of her good blouse, Rina felt its presence and heard it call to her, she heard its gentle voice, the cadence of the sound reached deep within her, and she understood somehow, that the Pendant had to be above ground.

She gazed at her Gram's closed eyes and heard the weakest of whispers steal into her mind, a winsome spiral of mist reaching out to her: "Keep it safe my gal, my chavvi, 'tis one of the keys, you'm gonna need it one day, pay me heed my babe."

"The Pendant needs me, Mam," was all she said.

Her Mother turned from her vigil at Gram's side sharply, and for a moment her blue eyes drilled into her, holding her captive with their intensity, "do it my chavvi?" she said finally, her head on one side, nodding slightly to herself. "Well best we let it be with you then." She smiled and the hesitant, questioning, hint of a sparkle lit up her face, "You, you … caught Gram's stream then?" she asked softly, expectantly. Rina smiled back joyfully, "Yes Mam, just now, I caught it," and she laughed out loud as her Mother jumped from the bench and caught her tightly in her arms, exclaiming aloud with pleasure. Outside, the others raised their faces to the sun and murmured their thanks to the Spirits, while the sentient rooks looked on cawing their approval.

The funeral took place two days later in the churchyard where Gram's husband Joseph, Mam's Father, my Gramps, was buried. Gram's Mother had also been buried there and several cousins. She would not be alone.

The service was serene and Lylie, Tommy and Rina were both saddened and uplifted by the knowledge that Gram was still with them albeit in spirit.

The Romanies stood dozens deep, silent and reverential. Gram had been much respected across the communities and gifts of food and punch were brought back to the glen for a celebration of her life. Gram's vardo was burned that night, in the river set back from the glen, while the stars above shone brightly and the roosting crows kept guard alongside the Watcher and his dog.

The next year passed slowly, and Gram's headstone in the shape of a gate to allow her access to her new life, was placed. Her mystic ball and cup and saucer were placed daily on her grave while visitors came and spent time telling her of their days, and keeping her up to date with their family news.

Slowly the camp started to renew itself, the outpouring of emotion and the disablement of structure and presence, had been debilitating and unsettling. As tradition and respect would have it, no new matriarch would be selected until a full year had passed.

The early spring grass lent the graveyard a velvet jacket and with the dew coating the young shoots it was an almost otherworldly sight. Rina sat on her haunches, crouched next to Gram, her toes wet through her sandals. The smell of new life made her draw her breath in deeply to savour the moment; she knew she was doing it for them both, seeing for two people, feeling, and breathing for two. The early sun warmed her bare arms, as she gently eased a money spider back onto the damp earth, watching as his tiny, delicate body disappeared into the grass.

Her eyes were misty, maybe there just weren't any tears left. She still missed her Gram so much it was a physical pain, and although she had hoped and prayed so hard, she had heard nothing from her since before the funeral nearly a full year ago.

Sighing she gazed at the Pendant lying on top of the grave, Mam would visit later with the other belongings. She, herself, was early today, the bird song had woken her, and she'd crept away before the others were roused, dragging her dress over her curls, and rubbing the sleep from her eyes carelessly. Stealing down the van steps she paused to see if anyone would note she was gone, she wanted this time alone.

Only the Watcher saw her go, his hooded eyes following her movements out of camp, as he made his way to set wood on the sleepy heart fire with dexterous fingers, teasing the embers, charming the small flickers of flame. Abruptly as the fire soared, he straightened his back unhurriedly, frowning slightly, watching, as his dog stiffened beside him, and the horses snickered and shuffled uncertainly under the budding trees.

"… and it turned out it was our old favourite Meadowsweet Gram." Rina lay with her chin on her hands chatting away, the velvet trimmed grave glinting beside her. She smiled happily at the thought of her growing knowledge and appreciation of the plants and herbs that her Gram had been teaching her. Her Mam was schooling her at this time, and she was working even harder now that her Gram wasn't here; she was doing it for her, so she would be proud.

Her Mam looked at her with such love in her eyes when she could pick out and name all the herbs and their uses, she knew Lylie was doing it for her own Mam too. Following the old ways gave them a purpose, something to cling to when the grief wracked their bodies and drained strength from their limbs.

"Me and Mam saw the primroses yesterday, Gram, we got a few roots, they're young and fresh. I can't wait for the flowers, there's lots of plants mind you. Mam was sad when we found them, but I wasn't, I was glad, I thought about what you said, and got the roots early." Mam had nodded when Rina said she wanted the young roots. "Yes, my babe, get them now lest they get bitter," she'd smiled but sadness had clouded her eyes.

"So, we dug 'em Gram, I …." A sudden nippy wind purled around her face, causing her to raise her eyes in surprise, but the sky above was clear and blue, the tree tops steady. Confused, she raised herself on her elbows, drawn to peer behind her; the grass leading right down to the lynch gate was clear. Turning back, she startled badly, a dark, slender figure stood just a few feet away and even in her confusion she wondered how he could have got so close without her noticing.

"Hello gal," a musical voice flowed towards her, and despite the warmth of the day, Rina shivered, her contentment receding. She lay still, her eyes wary, her fingers starting to burrow into the new grass involuntarily. And she knew.

"Why, … why are you back, Mister?" she murmured weakly through suddenly dry lips, her body filling with dread. "Do they know you're back; does *he* know?" she waited, hardly breathing. A slow smile lit the shadowed face, and the reply chilled her once again. "Just me and you, my gal, that's all who needs to know right now," he stifled a chuckle and she drew herself back trying to distance herself, readying herself for flight. He straightened his body and she suddenly noticed how tall he really was.

The saliva dried suddenly in her mouth, and fear crept insidiously down the back of her neck, the goosebumps rising on her skin, as her breathing quickened. '*Oh, Gram help me, what now, what do I do?*'

The tears were building in her eyes when the warmth suddenly reached her notice, and as the figure turned infinitesimally to check he was still alone with her she eased her eyes to the source of the heat as calmly as she could.

The Pendant was glowing sharply against the green of the grave top, and stifling her gasp, she moved her hand quickly and placed it on top of the stone, sliding it towards her in a swift, silent motion. "Be still now, my chavvi," cautioned her Gram's voice, a familiar love streaming to her, silent inside her head. "Don't let him see it, hold it close to you, he won't sense it then." Her voice faded and it was as much as Rina could do, to not cry out to her and call her back. Raising her eyes, she could see he was gone, just a chill persisted in the air to suggest his presence, or maybe the cold was just in her.

The creak of the lynch gate reached her ears, and she turned her head swiftly, to see the Watcher approaching her across the grass. "He's back, ain't he?" he asked flatly, squinting across the empty graveyard. "Are you ok, maid"?

Flinging herself off the ground she ran towards him, stumbling on numb legs, to throw her arms around his hard waist, burying her face in his body and welcoming the beat of his heart, solid beneath his old waistcoat, smelling of horses and fresh hay. "Yes Po," she whispered scratchily, and raising her head to gaze into his weatherworn face said apprehensively, "Yes, he's come back."

The summit later around the heart fire was sombre, the dark faces emotionless as they waited for Lylie and Tommy to speak their minds. The Watcher waited too, standing silently beside Rina, his heart twisted with the shame he always carried deep within him. His choices had been made long ago, but they still cut deep nonetheless, the emotional scars showing on his worn skin as the firelight flickered across his face.

When Lylie stood to speak to her people, even the air stilled in expectation. A collective intake of breath could be heard around the camp, and they raised their dark, gleaming eyes, waiting for the words that would set them all on the next course of their journey.

She stood tall and proud, her bearing almost regal, her wavy blond hair tied low on the base of her neck. Tommy stood beside her, feet apart, his stance that of a man confident in her words, his shirt white against the dusk light, boots scuffed and worn.

The course of action decided between the two of them, had been made, this was how it would be and all present would heed her words without doubt. Lylie and Tommy's choices would be in their best interests, their faith was unshakeable.

"Your new Matriarch will take her place," she paused and dipping her head, her eyes closed, she waited for the hum of excitement to die before murmuring, "she will abide by our laws, and our ways, she will uphold our honour and she will lead us strong and true until the day her last breath leaves her body."

She lifted her head high, "And we will lead her, guide her and protect her amidst us all, for the rest of our lives." The camp breathed expectantly, and all looked to Lylie and Tommy, waiting for their next words of affirmation.

"Rina, my darling, come here to me." Rina moved to her Mam's side ready for the unity which came with having her Mam made Matriarch of the Romany community, a most treasured and respected honour. She looked up at her with eyes full of love and pride and clung tight to her outstretched hand, while Tommy strode to Rina's other side, bending down to allow his arm to circle her young shoulders.

"Rina Pentham Stoneham," she called out unsteadily, her voice filled with a mix of emotions, "I bestow upon your shoulders, the mantle of Matriarch, to lead us forward on our path of honour, truth and freedom, to hear us all and mind our ways as the true guardian of the Romany people."

Lylie looked deeply into Rina's astonished face, and reaching for her, gently pulled the Pendant from beneath the neck of her dress, laying it carefully on her chest. She called out: "May all the Spirits protect her, may she cherish wisdom, kindness and truth. May she find loyalty, honesty, and love in all she does. Let her be our certainty and our compass, our journey, and our destiny, until the time of her passing decrees different. My Rina," she spoke gently, looking deep into her daughter's eyes, "there is nothing but good in your soul. You are here as you are meant to be, both by birth right, and by decree of the Pendant; catching the stream of the last living Matriarch further dictated this truth. It is, as it is meant to be."

A murmur of approval started to rise from the lips of the assembled Romanies, building and spiralling high into the night sky, while the fire leapt tall, its flames illuminating the joyful faces as after a full year of loss, the Romany people could finally embrace their new dawn.

Chapter 14 – 1957 – Po

He woke suddenly again, his body wet with sweat, his heart racing in his chest. The van seemed darker, the shadows denser, even than before. The dog snuffled on his rope outside, knowing his master was ill at ease. It was getting worse, every night now, every night a torment with the dreams, and he knew that he could put it off no longer, he would have to speak soon.

He wondered how much sadness and shame a body could take.

Sighing deeply, he promised himself: *tomorrow, I will speak tomorrow.* He rested his weary head on the pillow and at last fell into a peaceful sleep.

Rina rose with the dawn, the best of the mushrooms would be in the cool of the morning, when the dew lay heavy on the grass. She would get them into the village ready for the mealtime trade if she made good time.

She threw on her dress and ran her fingers deftly through the waves of her hair, letting it fall thickly down her back for warmth. Wrapping a shawl around her shoulders and knotting it at her waist she pulled on her shoes and made her way outside, down the steps of her van, only stopping to splash her face from the bowl and wipe it dry with the towel.

Picking up her basket she stopped for a moment to appreciate the mist lying low on the meadow beyond the glen, and the clean cold air hitting her cheeks.

"Wait, my gal," came a hoarse voice, out of the quiet, "I …. need some of your time today, if you have it?" He stood tall, his bearing proud, but she could see in the fall of his shoulders that the day had come that they had all been waiting for. "Po" she exclaimed kindly, albeit with well-hidden trepidation, "walk with me then, let's talk as we go."

She knew what it had cost the man to come to her, they'd all known it was just a matter of time, but out of respect for his pride, they had left him to approach her in his own good time.

They picked their way across the meadow, the river gurgling across the old granite stones, prattling and whispering in the dawn light. The dew soaked their shoes right through, but the chill of the air was refreshing and made her at least, feel alive. She could only imagine how Po felt.

She waited for him without comment, and after a while when the silence stretched on, she began to think that she had been wrong, that maybe today wouldn't be the day after all, and, she decided, if it wasn't, well then, they would all wait.

"Maid," he finally croaked, and her heart broke for him, how though could she make it easier without offending his dignity? "Po, I.." she started, but he cut in quickly, as though frightened the moment would pass, and his courage would fade.

"Daniel," he faltered, brokenly, how long had it been since he'd uttered his son's name she wondered? "Maid, I should have spoke before, but … but I was ashamed and I couldn't bring myself to say the words." He held his head low and she let him be. Sighing, he looked, up his mind somewhere else, long ago, and she could see the pain it cost him to remember.

Gathering himself, and shaking his head wearily, he forged on, and she kept him walking, hoping it would be easier that way.

"The day that Daniel got took away, well, we thought it was the worst day of our lives. My Sal never got over it, she was broken and we both thought that it was the hardest thing that we would ever have to live with." He sighed and turning to look into her eyes, he said brokenly, "We was wrong gal, it weren't.

"When we found out what he really done, well that was what finished his Mam, she didn't live to see the year out, bless her heart, the disgrace did for her. Y'see, I'll tell you how it was, maid, so's you understand why; why it's come to this, and why there's such fear.

"Jo, your Grampa had gone to work on Pitters Farm, the old man and Jo was mates from years back, and Jo had gone to do him some rouging, he asked Daniel to go along but he was a lazy one, and he never got himself out of bed in time, so Jo went alone."

Rina veered off purposefully to pick a mushroom and give Po a moment to collect himself, pulling aside the drenched grass, she plucked three glistening mushrooms, decked in dew, and placing them in her basket carefully, she looked up at him briefly and nodded him on.

"Daniel followed on a few hours later and Jo were out in the fields, far out of sight and so Daniel, well, he just laid himself down in the barn, smoking and plotting no doubt," he said bitterly.

Haltingly he continued "Pitter's daughter went to the barn, to fetch the eggs, she'd left it late and her Pa was proper mad with her so when she came into the barn and seen Daniel, well in a fit of temper aginst her Pa, well she gave the boy the time of day, and well, he…. well, he sweet talked her right back, and before she knew what happened he'd, he'd taken the maid down, he'd bedded her."

Po swallowed heavily, "The bugger, the bloody bugger; he ruined her. He charmed her, see; he used something precious, and charmed her, she was so struck with him, well he took advantage. He raped her, gal. She never knew what he was doin', she weren't in her right mind."

He looked off into the distance and taking his pipe out of his pocket lit it with two old flints without pausing. He turned as his dog bounded up to him, and he leant to rub his head roughly with calloused hands.

"That charm he used, it … it was the Pendant," and he nodded despairingly at Rina's gasp of dismay. "Yep, that's how he was able to take advantage," he continued bitterly, "he charmed her with the Pendant, and she didn't know what way was up. Poor little gal was done for, and she never was right in her head afterwards, she couldn't recollect nothing of any use."

He paused, clearing his throat; he wasn't used to talking so much. In all the years since, he'd kept his own counsel, too humiliated to make small talk and too ashamed to become much of a friend to anyone; firmly believing that he alone was responsible for his son's dishonour.

"Then," he continued quietly, "after the maid 'ad run from him, he took a flame and burnt the barn to the ground, with the animals still inside, they cried and screamed and Jo came running, but the heat was too much."

Ashen, Rina turned to look at him, but this time he couldn't meet her eyes. He ploughed on in anguish, "He came back to us, and swore black was white he never went near, but I knew, I knew it was him, God forgive him. Jo was none the wiser, but I said 'Daniel, I seen you' and he thought I had, so he couldn't deny it no more."

Turning he put an unsteady hand up to his mouth to wipe away the spittle. "He never would have put the Pendant back, but I took it off him, in his sleep that night. That bugger could still sleep after all he'd done, and I returned it to your Gran. She never spoke a word, but her eyes, dear God, her eyes. They was filled with such sadness, it near broke my heart.

"But Daniel, he had to go. I knew what I had to do, there was no choice, so I broke both our hearts, me and Sal, and I turned the boy in to the Gavvers, he got put away, gal, he was away for near on 12 year."

He stumbled on, the words nearly choking him. "The little maid, she was never right again, and when old Pitter found out, he put two and two together and he turned on your Grampa quick as you like, cursing and swearing at him, threatening him; and he got the locals so riled up, they chased us off the land with guns and sticks, threatening to burn our vans to the ground while we slept, chavvies an' all."

Running his hand down his face he went on, "We had to flee; with no time to do it right, we'd been on that site for near on sixty years. Jo was just about finished by it all, he couldn't hold his head up for the rest of his days, the shame; the thought that one of his own could treat a young maid like that, and ill-use a friend, someone who trusted us and we'd known for years, well it near killed him."

Turning away from her he could hardly continue through the knots in his throat, the humiliation tearing him up. "That boy he's a bad un through and through, my gal." He wiped the tears from his weathered cheeks with a shaking hand before continuing, "and now he's back, he's bin back this while, biding his time, but he's closing in, I can feel his wrath, and I'm afraid for you maid, I'm afraid for all of us."

Chapter 15 – 1958 – The Guardians

Rina had felt his presence, a brooding disquiet, laced with malice, his aura black, but even if she hadn't felt it, the leaves in Gram's cup had given warning years ago. The day of Gram's death suddenly came flooding back to her, and she caught her breath, gasping as the pangs of grief burrowed deep into her stomach, once again. She recollected the cup and leaves, the current of danger, and span of the ripples, the signs of death.

She knew this would go on and on, the prophecy travelling through the ages, touching them all, creating confusion, disorder and worse, much worse; meaning whatever action they took tonight would just buy them time. Raising her eyes to heaven, her lips trembling, she prayed for answers, for the way forward, and the rooks called back to her, giving her the response, they all already knew.

Drawing in a shuddering breath, it was all she could do not to run and hide. But for the love of them all, she held her ground, knowing that all she could do, somehow, *'but how, how, how, please help me Gram'*, was limit the harm, for now. She shivered into the chilly morning air.

The Pendant lay still and silent about her neck, she had caught no stream from her Gram since the day at the grave, years ago now. What to do, how to lead the people when they didn't know where, or truthfully when, he would show his face and deal his hand. Shaking her head, she voiced his name in her head – Daniel. She rested her chin on her hand as she sat on her stool, gazing into a blurry distance, trying to formulate some sort of plan.

The camp had risen early, with Tommy lighting the heart fire as Po watched on silently. The others went about their daily chores, talking to each other in short terse sentences, the tension palpable, while the children played half-heartedly amongst the trees edging the glen.

The rooks watched Rina silently, their bright black eyes boring into her, heads tipped to the side, eavesdropping. Looking up she called out to them, "Hroc, I can't do this, not on my own. Go, go tell my Gram I need her." There was an outside chance they could reach her she guessed. The birds stilled a moment, before with a heavy ripple of air, a party rose as one into the morning sky, circling the camp and cawing in their gravelly voices, as they went about their errand.

How could he be stopped? What could they do? Day and night the questions had plagued her, gnawing continuously, giving her little sleep and no peace.

Lylie and Tommy were worried sick and spent their days and nights, alongside the rest of the camp wondering what Daniel would do to initiate the prophesy. Asking themselves how they could ever hope to change what was already written.

It was as bad a time as it could be for Daniel to make his move. Lylie was almost due her second child, a baby that she and Tommy had wanted for so many years and were so excited about.

Rina glanced across, Lylie stood beside her wash stand, her belly huge, eyes shadowed as she scanned the camp, her hand absently stroking the new life she carried. She was nervous and skittish, spending her days jumping at shadows; she needed reassurance, and she looked for her Mam in every shawled woman she saw, but still the Pendant and Gram stayed silent.

Across the camp, Po and her Father stood together, side by side. Tommy lean and upright, as tanned and handsome as he was brooding. Po talked to him quietly under his breath, his hands moving expressively, pointing around the perimeter of the camp; she guessed to discuss setting up some kind of protection for tonight.

Since he had sought Rina out and unburdened himself, his shoulders seemed slightly broader, his seamed face a little lighter. The others had welcomed him back with open arms from his self-inflicted limbo, treating him with the same deference and respect that had always shaped their relationship, even if over past years Po could not bring himself to accept their overtures.

Today, his face battled fear, his breathing shallow, all present could feel his anguish. Long years had passed since he had last set eyes on his son and tonight, they all knew, would bring a reckoning.

Shaking herself mentally, Rina bade her anger rise: the indecisiveness had to stop, *of course* she feared for them all, all those who had stood together and forced this reckoning, those who had sealed his fate and taken his freedom.

Undeniably she was afraid to make a decision, but she *had* to plan, *take* advice, *call* a council and she *had to do it now*, before her sister was born, before they became even more vulnerable and had even more to lose.

The fire leapt, shadows playing on the faces of the Romanies as they took their places in the council circle later that evening. Clasping work worn hands in unity, dark heads bowed, they silently prayed to the spirits, thanking them for their presence at their fire, asking for their guidance this night.

The wind rustled through the trees, the dying leaves lifting in small vortexes, dancing in the nippy, dusk light; only pausing in their merry making to listen as an owl screeched its greeting.

The encampment waited silently, knowing that tonight the die would be cast, for better or for worse. Tonight, they were agreed, they were calling to the Materfamilias past and present, rousing the Old Souls, the Seraphs, and the Guardians, for tonight they would speak with the dead.

Gripping the Pendant in both her clammy hands, Rina stood in the centre of the circle, watched by her Mam and Dad, Po and the others, their collective breaths icy mists issuing from solemn mouths, dark eyes, unflinching.

The heart fire burnt low, the embers hardly glowing, while above them the returned rooks watched on soundlessly, keeping their guard as loyal sentinels of the night ahead. Bats swooped low beneath the tree line on the edges of the glen, as the midges danced around them in frenzied clusters of ordered chaos. The babes slept tight in the vans, swaddled and contented in their chamomile and lavender induced sleep.

As the Pendant in her hands started to warm, Rina, her heart bursting in her chest, began the incantations, passed down through generations of her ancestors, her young voice sounding out across the night, echoing off the trees, slicing through the night air and soaring like a winged bird across the meadow, before gliding back to her and wrapping itself around her body akin to a silvery mantle glistening in the fresh night air.

'Elders, I call to thee, Materfamilias, Seraphs, Old Souls and Guardians, approach our table, share our fire, for tonight we request your guidance. We beg you wake from your

otherworldly sleep and grace us with your presence, allow us your instruction, for we find ourselves in dire need of your aid. Come wake, rise, sit with your people, lend us your counsel, we the Romanies call to you.

Rina bowed her head low feeling the burning of the Pendant between her fingers as a distant hum, the slightest of vibrations issued beneath her feet.

Lifting her eyes, she stared transfixed as she saw the embers of the heart fire start to glow molten. The flames grew higher and higher still with every passing second, illuminating the camp and the faces of the assembled Romanies as the hum increased to an almost impossible crescendo, filling the glen with strange and unsettling tremors.

The wind had dropped and all other sounds were drowned out, as the feet high flames, started an improbable and dyslectic dance, reaching out almost to her hands before drawing back and gaining succour to reach her, yet again.

As suddenly as they had risen, the flames dropped, and the tremors eased. In the tranquillity of the moment Rina turned to look at Lylie and Tommy. Their faces were eery in the semi light, she saw sweat glistening on Lylie's face, her eyes wild and unfocussed, Tommy holding her fast; her fear increasing, she turned to Po whose body was upright and rigid, his eyes unseeing. Her gasp went unheard as a voice both powerful and strident, yet compassionate, issued from his lips.

"We answer your call our family."

From the edges of the River Meadow shadowy figures rose up from the earth, ethereal and wraithlike, their bodies translucent. They wended their way from the outskirts, heads held high, graceful and beautiful. Their auras surrounded them in soft spectral colours encasing their bodies with energy and strength, their voices humming sweet wordless enchantments, which floated gently on the night air.

"Mam," an elated voice suddenly cried from the darkness. "Oh Mam," and Rina saw Lylie fall heavily to her knees, holding out her arms imploringly as a beautiful wraithlike figure enclosed her in an otherworldly mist. Her eyes full, she watched enthralled as her Mam wept, tears of loss, desolation and finally joy, as her broken sobs quieted in her Mother's ghostly embrace.

The others surrounded the Romanies, reaching out to caress or embrace each and every one, lending their strength and love, filling them with a contentment that reached far beyond the physical body.

Uplifted and joyous, the Romanies turned childlike faces to each other, eyes shining as tears coursed down their dark cheeks, unashamed in their emotion, elated in their experience. They knew they would live with this night for the rest of their lives.

Rina felt, rather than heard her Gram. Turning she bowed her head as the tears fell from her eyes unheeded, and a familiar love washed over her. Closing her eyes she absorbed every bit of it, holding it deep inside her, knowing she would revisit it over and over again as the years went by.

A deep contentment seemed to reach her very core, entering every cell of her body and she gave herself up to the feeling, allowing her Gram's essence to seep into her body and mind, filling her with both courage and knowledge and suddenly she heard what her Gram was saying to her,

"My chavvi, my babe, he will come, the Traveller who is, and who isn't. He's not one of us, not a Romany, but a good man. Place your trust in him, he will hold it dear.

"You must wait my chavvi, and you'll know, you'll know when it's right. The right time to take action. You will know him as though you had always known him, he will be your future."

Chapter 16 – The Present – Lorentree Cottage

My sisters were both staring at me when I stopped for breath. I'd like to think they were spellbound by the wonderous powers of my story telling, but more likely it was with disbelief; I couldn't say with any certainty.

Considering how to break the silence, I took a gulp of my drink and glanced to Jon for his input. He though, damn him, sat silently, watching the fire dance, his wine glass nearly full, and tipped very slightly to the side, in danger of spilling all over the arm of the old squashy chair he was ensconced in.

As the silence dragged on, I licked my lips in preparation for …. for something to say, but truthfully, what was there to say, it felt like everything was balanced precariously, ready to rise or fall in the next few moments, and how the girls would react.

As a log fell in the fire, sending up showers of sparks, Libby finally spoke, and clearing her throat said weakly, "So, Sis, this is it, *this* is the secret you've been keeping from us all this time?" She looked at me, shaking her head almost imperceptibly, her eyes full of something I couldn't gauge, and because of that I was unsure of how to pitch my answer.

Elsie sat, unreadable, beside her, her whole body still, waiting for my response.

Sighing, I opened my mouth to speak, when Jon lifted his head, the movement causing me to falter. I looked at him with curiosity, how was he going to manage this? Dragging his eyes unhurriedly from the fire and looking over to the sofa where both the girls sat, he said slowly, "It's just *some* of the secret Libby, Elsie, there's more, much more to tell."

Including them both in his serious and questioning look, he asked, considering, "Do you want her to continue, there's no shame in letting all this go, we can forget about the whys and wherefores, we need never speak of it again. It can stop right now, just say the word."

"For God's sake, no!" interjected Elsie with split second, impatient, timing, "This is the most interested I've been in anything for the last God knows how many years." Turning to Libby she went on, "In for a penny, eh? We pushed for this," she said looking at her intently, "and now we're hearing the answers, what; we don't like them? No," she nodded firmly, "my vote is we plough on, let's hear everything, from beginning to end, we need to know what's going on, and why, we do, don't you think, sis?"

Turning further towards Libby, she put an encouraging hand on her shoulder adding: "Come *on* Libby, we can't help Anna unless we know what we're helping with and why, now, can we?"

We all looked towards Libby, waiting on her answer. Her blonde hair shimmered in the flickering light of the fire and suddenly seemingly without thought, Jon waved a languorous hand in the air and a hefty log flew into the fireplace, sending out monstrous licks of flame and embers. Elsie and Libby gasped, their gazes flashing towards him, like rabbits caught in the headlights. "*Jon!*" I hissed, knowing only too well that he never did anything without considering all the angles, but really?

"It's not a story, girls," he said ignoring me, "don't go thinking this is some sort of fairy tale Anna's spouting to you, this is real, it's dangerous and we," he looked over at me, "we, Anna and I, are in up to our necks. If you want us to continue, just know you *will* become involved. You *will* both have a part to play." He continued on more gently, "Again, I'm asking you both, do you want to hear more, or don't you?"

As the clock ticked, even the room seemed to hold its breath; minutes passed and the tension grew.

Libby moved suddenly, making us jump, and reaching for her baccy said serenely, "I'm in, you lot," and pushing herself out of the enfold of the old sofa, while leaving us amazed at her calm, crossed the flags to the front door, adding crisply, just as she departed into the darkness, "I only came out 'cos I thought Anna'd ballsed up in the office again!"

"Charming," I muttered, a relieved smile swamping my entire face. "Oh, it's not that easy Sis," Elsie said quietly, wiping away the relief instantly, "there are so many questions, I don't even know where to begin." She faltered into silence, clearly *not* sure where to start, and Jon spoke into the hush, "Everything you need to know we'll tell you, Elsie, but it will become clear when Anna continues, we'll leave nothing out I promise."

A waft of cold air hit the room as the door opened and a tousled Libby walked in, closing the door firmly behind her. "It's getting windy out there," she said calmly, and I looked across at Jon, meeting his eye long enough to catch his silent message: *'get on with it, Sis.'*

Chapter 17 – 1978 – River Meadow Cottage

It had been a long night for us all with what felt like, too much to process. We were all drained and emotional and with a residue of the headache still throbbing I could hardly keep my eyes open.

Mum called a halt to the story telling with a brisk, "Enough now kids, time to get some shut eye. Samuel, you move the girls out of our bed, the rest of you get to bed, you need to sleep," and before they left, without even knowing it had happened, I fell into a deep sleep, a wonderful heavy limbed feeling washing over me, a sweet oblivion after the events we had been through.

The darkness came later, with a sickening swirl of nausea hitting me so hard I found myself retching in my sleep, sitting up abruptly, the sheets tangled around my sweating body, my blurred eyes searching the room, probing for understanding, and settling finally, with dread filled recognition on a dark shadow standing in the doorway of the room.

God all bloody mighty, I realised with horror, Bris, was standing there, watching me.

The half-light of the landing, where Jon slept, outlined the figure, his face still in darkness, his silhouette nightmarishly chilling in the dim light, his malicious intent completely obvious; a feeling so very alien in the usually benevolent atmosphere of River Meadow Cottage.

I could feel fingers of malice twisting towards me, coiling and seeking, hunting silently and stealthily. My agitated breaths froze mistily in front of my face, almost, but not entirely obscuring the figure from my view. I couldn't move my paralysed limbs, so frozen in fear was I.

Then, just as the foul tendrils reached out to touch me, a small voice shrilled angrily from the bottom bunk, "Anna, dat man was in our garden and he upsetted my Mummy," and with a hurried scrunch of blankets, a glint of crisp white sheet, my little sister Libby, launched herself out of the bottom bunk, sleep- staggered over to the disconcerted figure and kicked him hard and unwaveringly on both his shins. Shaking her tiny finger up at him ferociously she hissed venomously,

"You a bad man." He drew himself taller in the darkness, startled and unfocussed, anger radiating from his body. "Don't you be here in my house, and push my Mummy over," Libby continued indignantly, "home time now, go on, home! …" and her small voice rose in such a furious shriek of outrage that it frightened even me.

In the next moment the bedroom door flew open, and Dad appeared, ruffled and bleary eyed, wearing an odd pair of spotted pyjama bottoms and wielding what looked very much like one of Granny Lylie's old walking sticks.

Suddenly, as he took in the situation: the dark menacing figure standing there, tense and coiled, Libby, hands on hips, glaring furiously upwards, Dad's eyes widened, and his stature changed almost imperceptibly. His body straightened and grew taller, his shoulders broadening and hardening in an almost neanderthal way, it was instantaneous and to me shockingly implausible.

From stern, narrowed lips an incongruous voice issued, breathing strange words, words with a dream like quality, musical and lilting, the cadence smooth and rich, the sounds unrecognisable, all the while the end of Gran's walking stick rose and fell, circling in the air, it's tip seeming to warm the motes around it, until a vortex of warm, yellow light surrounded the dark, solitary figure, eating into the struggling and hissing, dark wickedness, and little by little absorbing the awful shadow, diminishing the horrifying creature, until nothing remained.

A heavy silence filled River Meadow Cottage until a few seconds later, a shaky, voice came out of the darkness, "Why didn't I know, Samuel?" and Mum, her face distraught, stepped into the light of the landing.

Before Dad could answer a voice broke into the moment; "You were asleep, Mum," Jon's voice soothed gently, "you can't be the only one that keeps us safe." He spoke more firmly then, putting his hand on her arm from his bed, "We need a plan, don't we, because we aren't safe anymore, not here, probably not anywhere, who knows?"

Mum's eyes rested on him for a moment, and seemingly his words centred her. "Okay, yes, but I just don't know what that plan could be, and I'm not sure it can wait. After this I think we really need to talk right away." Not one of us could argue with that logic.

As the sun rose over the chestnut trees in front of River Meadow Cottage, we gathered, the girls and all. Binny, fresh from her undisturbed sleep in the caravan, wrapped in a blanket, her raven hair dark against the dawn light, led us purposely through the dew drenched grass to the meadow, to the hollow crater beneath the unused railway track overlooking the meadow.

As we stumbled along, I saw us with a stranger's eyes just for a moment. What an odd family I couldn't help thinking, such an unconventional group of ill clad people. I looked in wonder, here we were, dishevelled and unkempt, wrapped in blankets, pyjama legged, the girls clutching Beanie Boy and Gristlehound, chatting excitedly to each other.

Did we fit anywhere properly? How would my other school friends react if they could see me now? How could Mum, a member of the PTA, Dad, a sales Manager, fit into the other life, the real life? Or .... was it the 'real' life? I mused, suddenly filled with a sense of dislocation, what was 'real' or 'normal' and what wasn't? How many others were like us, keeping secrets, hiding .... abilities, fighting, as Libby termed it: 'bad men' and walking across dewy meadows at dawn to devise a plan to, what, *kill*, a .. an… *'evil*... what, *an evil adversary'*? Surreal. Shaking my head at the madness of it all, I walked on.

And finally, I wondered to myself, how Binny could have known that this place, the hollow beneath the disused railway line, surrounded by trees, was the only place we would be able to find sanctuary?

"We haven't much time," Dad started right away, once we were all sitting on our bin liners, wrapped up warm in the early morning light, cosy in the hollow. We'd sped to the kitchen with breakneck swiftness, made a flask of tea, and speedily picked up several of Mum's cookies: "I *need two*, Mum," Elsie had whinged plaintively, so in the interests of any sort of adult conversation being achieved, a huge handful of extra cookies had been added to the rucksack.

It was warm in the hollow, the scented earth and dappled light soothed our battered souls, and we relished the safety and acceptance of the space around us. Sitting on our blankets, tea in hand, chomping on biscuits, for a moment it was almost possible to forget why we needed this sanctuary.

Looking down reflectively, his face shadowed, Dad continued the story as though there had been no break in our conversation since the night after the party.

"We've told you about Rina on the night of the council, and Gram and how she helped Mum at the council," he said getting straight to the point. "Look this isn't going to be easy listening, but for us to make our own plan, you have to know the background, from beginning to end, as we lived it."

He looked at Mum briefly. "Your Mum will have to go from here, it's more about how she felt, what led to the decisions that were made, and how it was left. She won't leave anything out, but when she's finished, well then, that's when we may need to call our own council." Eyes wide we glanced around at each other; Jon's eyebrows were raised. "And then at the very least, we can keep ourselves out of danger, for now," he added.

"For now," I shrilled, in horror, "why only for now?" Dad looked back at me steadily. "Because," he said slowly, "this was predicted to affect generations, and we still don't know how to fix it, we can only stave it off. That's our best bet for the moment, keeping us safe right now is what matters most."

Chapter 18 – 1960 – Leaving Home

She looked at him intently, willing him to understand. She was telling him first; before even her man and Dad, they'd been through so much together, him and her. She loved him like a Father, and knowing what he'd been through, how battle scarred he was, she was loathe to cause him any more pain, but she knew this was something she had to do.

"Po," she started hesitantly; they were sitting on the log together side by side, next to the river. The water burbled behind them, calling to them and chiding them for not coming more often.

It was the very seat they'd taken together many a time; the time her Gram had died, the time Rose was born, when Daniel …. but suddenly his next words left her silent. "You'm going, maid, aint you?" He looked at her knowingly, eyes glittering, his voice low. "Oh Po," her voice wavered, as tears spilled from her eyes, dropping in a seemingly endless flow, onto her lap. "Hush, maid, shhh, it's alrite, gal, I sin this comin' a long while. You'm off to search for your man, I'm rite aint I?" He looked away from her into the distance. "Yes, Po," she whispered back brokenly, "you're right. Oh Po, I have to find him, he's not one of us you see. Gram told me; she said he wasn't, but she knew he was a good man, a Traveller, and he would be part of the prophecy." She looked at him intently, "Will you …?" "Yes, my gal, I'll be alrite," he said briskly, albeit a little hoarsely. "I bin through worse than saying, *'see you soon'*, to you. You gotta do this, maid, you gotta do what's written, and ifen he aint one of us, then you got to find him, gal. You go, and you be sure to bring him home." He turned his face away from her, "You'll … come back to me, then?" "Po, oh yes," she whispered to his bowed head, through her tears, "always, I'll always come back to you, Po, I love you." Turning his body away from her he uttered quietly, "You too, my maid, you'm my gal, always have bin, always will be."

"There's something else Po." Reaching for him, she took his calloused hand and clasped it tightly. "In my absence ..." "Yes maid," he said slowly, "I will be the Matriarch, in your absence only; until you feel ready, until he's found, I will take the mantle." She looked at him searchingly, and nodding her head lifted his hand to her lips. "Thank you," were the only words left to say.

Chapter 19 – 1960 – The Traveller

Probably the only words, in the whole world, that could have made a difference to her decision.

He stood before her smiling, his face a picture of mischief, but at the same time managing to look both vulnerable, charming and astoundingly familiar, all at once. She turned back to him, lost for words for a moment, and he repeated to her, "Will you come with us, don't you want to see the *fairies* at the bottom of my garden?"

Her laughter took her by surprise, it burbled from her, and felt so very unlike who she had become, *who she had needed to become,* she reminded herself quickly. Even so … she drew a breath in, ready to refuse, when he suddenly spoke again, pre-empting her answer. "Fi and Lou are coming and my brother, Arthur. You'll be safe I promise, and …" he spoke proudly then, "I have the car."

She smiled back at him, she had no choice he was so … so winning, that was the description of him, she finally settled on. She looked hard at him, trying to read his aura, and feeling the kindness, immediately by-passed that bit, and moved on to the real test. This would do the trick she thought, and surprisingly, she found she was disappointed at the thought of not going to 'see the fairies' with him and the others.

"I don't believe in *fairies,*" she lied heavily, and now for the piece de resistance, her 'go to' line; "and … my Father's a Romany, he wouldn't like it." Glumly she turned away, knowing that last sentence would have done the trick, as it always did.

Romanies were a proud race, known for their fierce adherence to their culture. Relationships outside of the community were never welcomed, and as for the Matriarch; well, she may as well just say goodbye to Samuel right now.

"Let's go and ask him then, shall we Katarina?" and even as she wondered how he knew her name, she let him take her gently by the hand and lead her towards the door of the dance hall.

Samuel, he was called Samuel, she knew that much. She had watched him all evening, flitting from person to person, and girl to girl, chatting and laughing, completely at ease. She had smiled at the warmth of his behaviour and watched with curiosity how the others had enjoyed his infectious company, his friendship. They had called to him as he left each group and made off laughing, to chat with another set of acquaintances; they wanted him back, needed his energy to complete their fun. It didn't hurt one bit that he was easy on the eye, she thought a trifle tetchily.

He'd spoken to Lou and Fi, her cousins, but as far as she could tell he didn't seem to look in her direction at all, and she carried on making small talk with some of the girls from work, whom she'd recently met. They were a good fun bunch and she found herself laughing out loud at some of the antics they told her about.

She'd landed a job in the Pottery in Ashburton, it was the job of her dreams, she spent her days painting delicate designs on the Pottery with other girls of her age. The process was painstaking and intense, just what she needed to keep her mind occupied. It was perfect, well almost perfect, she thought; it was as good as it was going to get anyway.

She was earning now, the little terrace they rented had an outside lav, just for them! She still went out at the end of the day; just to look at the wooden bench seat in the little brick lavatory at the end of the tiny garden, with wonder. How different her life was, she smiled sadly to herself: *this is what you wanted girl, you're doing it, keep searching.*

The cold night air hit her as he walked her through the front door of the old Guild Hall, holding tightly to her hand. *Funny how a hand can feel so right,* she'd thought fleetingly, wonderingly*: was it him? Could it be?*

The streetlights were shrouded in a light mizzle, their solitary eyes looking down on her, on them, and she wondered inanely, how her hair would look in a few moments. Would he still smile at her with that innocent pleasure, when it was plastered to her skull and dripping down into her eyelashes?

"Katarina, over here," Fi called out to her from across the way, leaning up against a vast dark car, her heels high and elegant in the light, her eyes shining with mischief. "Come on, slow coach, let's go for a ride, it's a lovely car, and the night is young!" She giggled happily, and Katarina, observing her pleasure, decided for once to let her guard down and throw caution to the wind.

"Your carriage awaits, mademoiselle," he looked into her eyes, smiling with such energy and enthusiasm it was contagious. Curious about him, perhaps more than that; maybe intrigued, she held out her hand, and he escorted her gallantly across the road, and opened the car door ceremoniously.

"Well, I'll be, it's a bus!" she exclaimed in surprise after they had driven a couple of miles up onto the moor just outside Ashburton. They pulled over into a rather tumbledown, grassed driveway just off the road, and stopped, the car shuddering to a noisy halt. She turned to him her eyes shining with query: "Is it yours? Is it your bus?"

Fi and Lou were chatting to Arthur, their voices high with excitement, and together they watched through the misted windows of the car, as smoke rose from an old, crooked stack, positioned on the roof of an ancient red, double decker bus. The windows were mainly all curtained against the night, but she could see lamps burning, throwing a warm light out onto the silhouetted trees surrounding a fairly large site.

"Of course," he said with a hint of pride, "I thought everyone knew, we've been here for ages."

"Well, I never," she half whispered to herself, of course it's a bus. So that's what Gram had meant; all these years and she still remembered, she always would, the words she'd absorbed on the night of the council, the night the guardians had risen.

"My chavvi, my babe, he will come, the traveller who is, and who isn't. He's not one of us, not a Romany, but a good man. Place your trust in him, he will hold it dear. You must wait my chavvi, and you'll know, you'll know when it's right. You will know him as though you had always known him."

She looked at him, sitting beside her in the car, quiet and patient, and waited for her thoughts to settle. "Do I know you?" she questioned shakily, "I feel … I feel like I already know you, Samuel." She didn't mind saying the words to him, didn't feel as though he would find her odd, odd and different maybe.

He answered carefully, as though he had to find the right words, words that would seal this moment, and maybe more. "Feasibly," he said with deliberation, "this is how it was always meant to be, Katarina?" He looked into her eyes intently, "I'm willing to try and find out, if you are." He held her gaze, his brown eyes still, his warmth reaching to her. "Yes," she said, "Yes, let's find out Samuel," and then … "please," and she let the smile she'd been guarding since she laid eyes on him, finally reach her face.

He was her secret, not from Fi and Lou, not from the girls at the pottery, but definitely, from her Mam and Dad. And anyway, what if she was wrong, what if he wasn't the one, what then? But she knew, she already knew, deep in her heart, he was the one her Gram had prophesised.

The month turned into two, and then three. Mostly they went places with the girls, it was always a party, or a picnic. It was walks on the moors, laughter when he got his leg stuck in a rock pool at Hope Cove, more laughter when he got caught trying to rescue a sparrow and inadvertently let it escape inside the car, turning the leather into a map of the world with the resulting panic induced bird poo. It had taken hours to get it clean, and the bird hadn't given him a backward glance when it flew, perfectly unharmed, off into the sunset.

She'd never felt so at peace, she woke every morning with a smile on her lips and the days flew by in a haze of happiness. It was almost like a wonderful dream, that she hoped she wouldn't ever wake from, but still, she could sense something coming. Something lurking on the horizon, and as much as she tried, it would not go away.

"The pictures? Yes, how lovely," she'd said happily, and then agreed shyly when he'd stressed it would just be the two of them. "I want to talk to you, Katarina," he'd told her gravely, and her heart had jumped with anticipation. Could it be, she'd wondered? After all, it had been nearly two years.

"It'll be for three months," he'd said quietly, looking into her eyes, and for just a moment she thought she must have misunderstood. "Sorry Samuel, what did you say?" she stuttered at him.

He'd looked at her, both sadly, but also, she realised, with a grim determination. "I'm going away, it's only three months darling, I'm going grape picking in France, a friend has organised it, we go next week. Now listen," he'd caught her hands in his, hurriedly, pre-empting the words she was actually incapable of uttering; such was the sense of loss that engulfed her, "now listen to me, we need this space, time to think, to make decisions, to ensure that if, no, no, not if, when, when, we move forward together, we will know it's what we both want. It's time darling, to let you decide what you want, do you understand?"

She was so upset, it hurt to breathe, devastated that he didn't already recognise how he felt, or how she felt about him, for that matter, that he didn't appear to understand that their fates were intertwined, were prophesied even. But before she could even put words to her wracking, gut twisting, disappointment, he continued,

"Now listen to me, I know what you're thinking darling, but listen, this isn't about me. This is about you."

She gaped at him speechless at the absurdity of his assumption and she suddenly realised that the premonition of unhappiness she'd been having, was this, this … *betrayal*.

"You have decisions to make, you must decide whether or not you are going to introduce me to your Father." He looked at her, his eyes unwavering, "I won't be your guilty secret for ever." *Oh God*, he *knew then, he'd known all along that she hadn't told them.* She lowered her eyes, wanting to blurt out the words; *but I will, I promise, I'll do it now, I'll do it now, right this minute Samuel, please, please don't leave me, don't go.* But he stopped her, his hand slightly raised, shaking his head, his mind made up. He continued stoically, his eyes shimmering in the darkness.

"The time has come for you to make your decision, and I am giving you the space to do it, without me here to pressure you, without me darling; because if you decide that you cannot, after all, face your Father, then you will have to decide not to see me again." His brown eyes searched hers sadly, gravely, and finally she saw the pain this had caused him, and she felt ashamed of herself, and more, she had caused him so much anguish. Abruptly, she saw his decision for what it really was, an honourable act, an act of selfless love, she looked at him, a small smile playing on her lips, her decision made. How she loved this man; the resolution surged through her veins, hot and determined. Tomorrow, she would go tomorrow, whether he went, or he stayed, no one was going to stand in the way of her and this man, not from now on, and never again.

Chapter 20 – 1962 – The Meeting

"Mr Stoneham, what a pleasure to meet you." Samuel paused just long enough to observe the tightening of the other man's lips, the strong, vicelike grip as they shook hands. "Katarina has been telling me about you, I'm glad that we've got this chance to meet and talk," he said, his voice strong, the light in his eyes sombre.

The man was stern, Samuel thought, he gave off a sense of honour and deep pride. "And Mrs Stoneham," he greeted Lylie, shaking her outstretched hand and taking in the almost hidden warning in her eyes. She was a lovely looking woman, he thought briefly; her blond wavy hair falling almost to her waist, her eyes a cornflower blue, she looked kind, which was a tad different to how Tommo seemed right now.

He turned his gaze to the man, assessing him, noting the tall, bronzed and sinewy form, his shirt sleeves were rolled up, dark wool trousers held up about his waist with a huge leather belt. He gave off an aura of power and resolve.

Samuel drew himself up continuing on calmly, "I wanted to take this opportunity to meet you, Sir, and introduce myself, to make you aware of my intentions towards Katarina, you see…."

"I already know your intentions, young man," Tommo cut in brusquely, his dark jaw tense. "I'm guessing, due to rumours hereabouts, that you want our *Rina* to be your wife." He looked into Samuel's eyes intently, as he stressed the Romany version of her name, "And I'm guessing you came here, to ask me for my daughter's hand, am I right?"

Samuel took a breath, straightening his shoulders, and when he spoke again his voice was strong and determined, his shoulders straight, "You are right, Mr Stoneham, quite right, that is why I'm here, I am, we, I should say, are hoping for your blessing to get married."

Katarina, sat on the bench outside of the vardo, her breathing rapid. The old heart fire burned low and across the glen she could see the others, keeping their distance, giving them the privacy they needed to get through this moment, and she was grateful to them.

Po stood alone by the horses, silent, biding his time, she guessed. Not for the first time she wondered how he really felt about her reasons for leaving.

As she started to rise, Tommo turned his stern gaze away from Samuel, "*Rina,*" he emphasised, "go with your Mam and you, Rose my chavvi, this is men's talk." Looking at her Dad silently, then sending a long, searching look to Samuel, she waited for his nod.

He smiled at her tightly, as she rose and took her Mam's outstretched hand, and catching hold of Rose with the other they made their way off in the opposite direction to the others, across the far side of the river meadow to the river.

She turned her eyes farther up the river to see Po give her a small nod of his head, a slight smile playing on his weathered lips; he was standing, straight and tall beside their log. He nodded once again, and seated himself deliberately on the old tree, looking straight into her eyes. "I'm here, my maid," she heard him send silently. She half raised her hand in acknowledgement, if this was all ok, if her Dad could only see … then she'd take Samuel to Po, and the thought brought her a brief flash of pure unadulterated joy, but for now all she could do was smile back at him weakly, tears brimming.

"Oh Mam, he's as bad as I thought he would be," she whispered to Lylie a few minutes later. The river, pleased to see her back, gurgled and chatted to her, but she was too tense to take note. They sat on the meadow grass, along from the small bridge, looking back to camp. Tommo and Samuel were squaring up, she could see it and her anxiety increased.

"Oh Mam."

Her Mam looked at her through gentle eyes, her hair dancing in the breeze, "It is as it will be my babe, all the worry in the world won't change it. Now come and hug your Mam, Gram will have sorted this out I daresay," and she smiled serenely at her eldest daughter, her faith in her own Mother so very certain.

"He's *him,* Mam, the one Gram told me about, the one she said was my future." Katarina stumbled to a tearful halt, releasing her hold on her Mam, "What if Dad won't see it, what if he won't give his consent, what then?" Lylie sighed deeply, "Oh, my babe, your Dad can see it, he just wants to be sure that your young man fights the good fight for you. After all, anything worth havin' is worth fighting for, isn't it?"

Smiling mischievously, she ruffled Rose's hair, "Isn't that right, my Rose?" Rose smiled up at her cheekily. "Samuel wants to marry me, instead of Rina, he told me just now, he said he would have waited for me, but Rina was getting all snarky!" The women looked at each other and laughed out loud, the tension in the air easing; and hugging Rose to her waist, Katarina begged all the angels that her Dad would be gentle with Samuel.

"*How much*?" he expelled finally, *grimly*, when the breath had come back into his lungs. "Mr Stoneham, Sir, are you *seriously* offering me money to leave Katarina alone? You can't be surely?" Samuel shook his head, as though to clear a fog. "Have I got that right; did you just offer me money to disappear out of her life?"

He squinted at the older man in utter disbelief, a sense of disappointment washing over him from head to toe. Not because her Father had said no, he hadn't, yet, anyway, but God he was hurt, what on earth did the man take him for? How shallow did Katarina's Father think he was? And what about the honour he'd attributed to Katarina's Father, how could he have read him so very wrongly? He wasn't proud and honourable, damn him, what Father would do this to his daughter? *And what now for God's sake?*

He rose slowly from the wooden seat outside the vardo, his anger rising like the tide. "What the hell sort of man do you take me for?" Samuel rasped, his shock leaving him strangled; he was dazed at the rage the older man had raised in him and beyond insulted at the characterisation afforded to him. "I love your daughter, with my *whole* heart, I want to *marry* her, to have a life with her, to have *children* together. I want Katarina to be ***my wife***.

"There is no money in this world that can buy me off. Do you understand me, *Mr* Stoneham, do you understand what I am saying?"

His voice broke slightly and as he started to turn, to go he didn't know where; so, he was staggered and momentarily infuriated, by the smile that suddenly lit up Tommo's handsome face.

"Stay your hand, my boy, no need to heed my words," he placated, "I just needed to be sure. I knew, lad, I saw from the minute my gal spoke your name, that you was the one; her eyes told me all I needed to know."

Standing up slowly, Tommo reached for Samuel's still rigid hand and grasping it firmly between his own said, "You have my blessing son, you take good care of my gal, my *Rina,*" and with tears streaming down his bronzed cheeks he turned and strode off across the glen towards the woods, his shoulders rigid, his head held high.

Chapter 21 – 1964 – Anna

"She can't be around the Pendant darling, we both know that," Samuel looked at her firmly, "we agreed didn't we, we have to do this. Look I know it's hard darling, but we can't chance it, surely you understand that, don't you?" He gazed at his wife despairingly, she looked beautiful he thought, her honey blonde hair, short now, curled around her neck, her blue eyes gazing down into the baby's face. He reached out to touch her cheek, and she lifted unhappy eyes to his, "Yes, I know Samuel, I do know; it's just so hard for me. I always knew it had to be above ground, right from when Gram went. I'm really struggling with the thought of burying it, it's like letting her down, breaking a promise."

"I know," he heaved a sigh, "I understand, but sometimes there isn't any other choice, we must keep Anna safe, she's our priority now. Maybe we can find another way in the future, but let's just keep her safe for now, how about that?" She nodded at him bleakly, but at least she nodded, and that was enough, he let out a silent sigh of relief.

They'd been drawn to River Meadow Cottage the moment they laid eyes on it. It called to them in ways they hadn't even realised existed.

River Meadow Cottage, their new home, had all the things they had ever dreamed of; two bedrooms, plus a big landing, an inside toilet and bath, separate kitchen, dining room and sitting room. It was all beams and fireplaces. Glossy luxurious thatch, much like a mane, covered the roof, surrounding the chimneys that jutted proudly into the night sky.

Outside in the lawned garden, young trees swayed and danced in the lightest of summer breezes, as the wild flowers competed with each other for space. Across the meadow, three chestnut trees lined a small brook running through the centre of the village, past Island House, so called because it got surrounded with water during the winter months.

High above the meadow, a disused railway track boasted ragwort and cow parsley during the summer months, and hazelnuts hung in abundance, along the sides of the old tracks during the autumn, but it also hid a further secret.

It was a dream home, but it was more than that, much more, it was a necessity, an obligation. There really was no choice.

They crossed the brook at the shallowest point the next morning. Anna in a sling on Katarina's chest, watched the leaves of the trees dapple in the sunlight, her blue eyes riveted. Samuel carried a large bag slung over one shoulder, his wellies squelching through the marshiest parts of the meadow underneath the rise of the redundant tracks above them.

Trees protected the secret hollow in the meadow, the sacred ground, but they knew where they were going. There must have been a part of them that had always known that this place would be their future, their sanctuary.

It looked impenetrable, a front of foliage standing lustrous, proud and strangely intimidating, almost invincible in its effort to protect what lay beyond. They had to force, with absolute determination, their way through the tangle of branches, brambles and grasses that grew with unprecedented strength high into the summer sky, with Samuel and Katarina shielding Anna's face from a prickly assault. It was almost impassable, and certainly not somewhere anyone else would just stumble upon.

Once they were through, in what seemed like hours later, scratched and sweaty, the hollow was surprisingly large. Dim from lack of light but warm and dry, the hollow greeted them kindly, welcoming them with a strong smell of loam and dried leaves. The floor was coated with a fine, dry soil, only the roots of the trees breaking the evenness of the surface. The silence was so profound, it was almost a noise.

"It's beautiful, isn't it?" breathed Katarina. "Just perfect." Samuel turned to look at her, his brown eyes searching hers, his fear subsiding just a little. She could do this, he thought, but his heart fell, yes, she could do it, of course she could; but at what cost? His stomach contracted anxiously, and there would be a cost, he knew that.

"It is a perfect hiding place, Katarina, dry, warm and sheltered through all weathers." He spoke gently, his hand reaching for hers. "The Pendant will be fine here. What's more we can keep an eye on things from River Meadow Cottage too, so you can rest easy, my love." *Oh, Samuel such easy words,* he thought.

She turned to look at him, a brave teasing lift to her lips, "Stop worrying darling, I'll be fine, Gram will understand; she'll want Anna safe, too." She smiled tightly, her face oozing love. "Get digging, Mr James, it's nearly lunch time!"

With shaking hands, they placed the Pendant in an old cigar box, which had once belonged to Pops, Samuel's Dad, wrapped tightly in tissue and a tea towel. Samuel touched her arm lightly, encouragingly, his brown eyes warm, and she lifted Anna's small hand to stroke the towel before closing the lid. Katarina's hand lingered wretchedly over the box before she finally passed it to him.

The hole was deep, deep enough to ensure that a single spade, plunged into the fine, dry soil, wouldn't find it. Deep enough to hide the pulse of the stone, to keep it from disturbing the balance of their lives, to ensure its powers were contained and couldn't be ill-used. Mostly, though, deep enough to prevent the Pendant assigning itself to the next generation, their new daughter, Anna, and any other children to follow.

All the way back to River Tree Cottage, her body longing to turn back, fighting to take every step away from the hollow, Katarina could hear the Pendant calling to her, its low melodious voice beseeching, pleading, begging.

She couldn't contain the tears that ran down her face, pooling in her blouse collar, soaking the cotton, and she couldn't stop her baby's head, turning continually to the direction they had just left, her neck stretching and straining backwards, towards the hollow, and wailing fiercely, her small fists clenched in misery.

The days and nights that followed were indescribably awful. Katarina was as unhappy as she had ever been; she felt she had broken her word to Gram and her Mam, reneged on something intangible. There seemed to be no respite from the constant, dragging shame of her actions.

Anna was a nightmare, fractious and irritable, inconsolable one minute, staring listlessly into space the next. The only sane one among them, although he didn't know how long that would last, was Samuel.

They stumbled through the week, somehow managing to eat, drink and maintain the minimum standard of cleanliness, but by the end of the last day they knew it couldn't go on. Something would have to give.

It did give, and it gave in the form of Lylie, followed closely by Tommo and Rose, walking down the garden path the following day, bag in hand, her long wavy hair fastened behind her in a thick lustrous plait, which swung jauntily as she walked.

"Hello, my babe," she called joyfully, "let me look at you," and she reached to hold her eldest child in her arms taking a moment to process what she saw.

Anyone with a shadow of understanding could see how Rina was faring, and it didn't look as though she was doing well, not well at all. Lylie, her arms around Rina, her chin resting on her head, felt a curious emptiness of spirit, a detachment, feelings she could not recall ever being a part of her eldest daughter before.

"Tommo," she called quickly, over her shoulder, trying to buy a little time, a split second to prepare for how she should deal with this situation. She was shocked and worried, by how drawn, haunted might be a better description, that Rina looked.

Tommo wasn't quite so restrained; looking like he'd been smacked in the face, he exclaimed instantly, "Dear God, chavvi, what's gone wrong? You look like you lost sixpence and found a penny! You'm wrecked maid."

"Daaaad," came Rose's scolding voice from behind him. "Say *hello* first". Katarina's weak chuckle was the first light-hearted sound she'd heard herself utter for a good week. "I'm alright, Dad," she threw a look over her shoulder. "Samuel come out, look who's here," and she turned to find him at her shoulder, his relief so transparent it brought a tender smile to her face.

"Tommo, Lylie, Rose," he said wholeheartedly "not a moment too soon, did you get my message then?" Katarina turned towards him questioningly, as Lylie replied, "Not a message from you, Samuel," and she smiled at Katarina lovingly, "Rina called for me."

Katarina flung herself into her Mam's arms, holding on for dear life, and Lylie, extricating herself, just enough to turn Rina towards the meadow spoke over her shoulder, "Time for a chat, us girls need a catchup, take me there, Rina. Rose, come on, my gal." Katarina looked at her for a moment before nodding her head and sighing resignedly, "This way, Mam."

The midday sun leant a warmth to the meadow and a breeze played artlessly around them as they made their way silently towards the hollow. Rina stiffened as she caught the first melodious tones, a call both plaintive and touching, the sadness of the sounds echoing her own misery, calling to her very soul.

Lylie walked on, her steps even, her face impassive, had she even heard anything Rina thought? Rose tilted her head to one side and a smile played on her lips.

"I'm going to come and look out for you," Rose said in a lilting voice, they both looked at her curiously. Her eyes were far away, her small face dreamy. "One day," she said, "I'm going to come and look out for you."

Rose shook herself, her face changing back to the mischievous child of a moment ago, "Can I explore, Mam?" Lylie and Rina looked at each other, momentarily side-tracked; "Yes, my babe," Lylie managed. "Explore, but only here with us, mind."

As they pushed their way through the thick foliage around the hollow, the air grew warmer and more still, the call increasing in volume. It was as much as Rina could do to not run over, fall to her knees, and dig her hands into the soil. Lylie looked at her daughter; Rina's face was the image of restraint, sadness absorbing her whole aura. She nodded to herself; they had been right to come straight to her.

"Dig it up, my babe," she said evenly, looking her daughter in the eye and continuing firmly, "Right now, this minute, you know this isn't how it was meant to be." "Mam," she cried desperately, "how can I? You know as well as I do what it will do to Anna. Surely, it's better this way, Anna will learn to live without it, it's safer for us all, isn't it?" Her eyes started welling and screwing them up briefly against the tide of emotion, Rina leaned towards her Mam. "What about them tracing us? What then?"

Her Mam took her by the shoulders and looking deep into her eyes said fiercely, "Use another way, you have the skill, gal, use your skill for the love of God. Look at you, look at all of you, you'm all wrecked, this can't go on, now can it?" She lowered her tone persuasively, lovingly, "Do it now my babe, don't waste another precious minute, 'cos this won't stop, it'll call to you for the rest of time, and you'll live a half-life, just trying to shut it out, and what for? So's you can stay safe from something that may never happen?"

"It'll happen anyway, whatever course you take," a young voice piped up. "It's written, isn't it?" Rose looked at them both. "Isn't it?" she said her voice questioning.

Rina looked back at Lylie, her mind working ten to the dozen, Rose was right, it would happen anyway it was written. So … could she, how about starting with weighing up the risks? Dare she do this? Hope started to blossom in her chest, and turning to her Mam she said quickly, "Can I find a way, d'you think Mam? How do I do it? I don't know how." "'Course you do," her Mam answered briskly. "Ask the Pendant, my babe, you just have to ask, there's always another way." She smiled with satisfaction, "The Pendant answers to you, surely you know that by now, just ask."

Katarina looked at her sighing, "It's not about the asking, Mam, it's about the tracing, as well you know; if it was that easy, I would have sorted it already. The Pendant can always find a way to be with me, with us, if I ask it to, but it won't be able to find a way to be untraceable."

"No, Rina, but you can, you can find a way, can't you?" asked Rose's eleven-year-old voice of wisdom.

Chapter 22 – 1959 – The Cleanse

It came to something didn't it, when the old man would consider bringing his gal to her? She'd not seen that coming, not in a month of Sundays. Glancing across the full but silent camp she caught Po's narrowed eyes, absorbing the scene in front of him. She sent back silently: *why are they here?* He hitched his shoulders, shaking his head at her, *no idea, but be careful maid, Tommo won't like this, don't make no promises, alrite?* Gazing at him a second longer she nodded slightly.

Raising her eyes to the girl sitting in front of her, she appraised her silently, her hands itching to reach out and stroke the waxen cheeks. The girl's blank eyes stared right through her, unseeing, the pupils dilated, haunted even. She looked like a shell of the happy young maid who'd played in the farmyard all those years ago. Her hands lay limp in her lap and a brush hadn't seen the tangle of her hair for many a long day.

What did they want from her now? Lylie thought resignedly. They'd left the site near the farm long ago, years ago. Left, she thought sadly, no not really, no; they'd been chased off like animals, but in all fairness, she reminded herself, who could blame old Pitter. Not her, not any of them, but what now, so many years had passed, what did they want now?

Glancing back at Po, she felt his pain, saw him remembering, the tension in his body causing the air to vibrate around him. The Others kept their dark eyes trained on her, making no secret of their intention, should it come to it.

Drawing her eyes back to the newcomers, she met the determined gaze of old man Pitter. His chin jutted at her defiantly, his eyes hard. He stood proud but keenly ravaged. He'd aged gravely in the past dozen years, his once strong and upright body, bowed. His sparse hair, clung to his skull, the pallor of his skin telling its own story to a healer such as her. She felt a swell of pity for his loss, for the life never lived by the maid in front of her. Her lips parted to speak to the girl in front of her, but she was surprised into silence.

"The boy done this," he spat suddenly, hostilely, "he done this to my gal." He pointed to his daughter; his rheumy eyes filled with the brightness of anger. "She ain't never bin right, poor maid, not since he … not since then. Look at her God damn you!" his voice rose higher in an old longstanding anguish, but as his eyes lost their heat, he lowered his voice, his strength lost with the energy of his outburst, "I'm right scared of how she is." The tremble of his hands increased and burying his hands deep in his pockets to hide his weakness he muttered desperately, "My gal, she, she needs help, Lylie. I can't think of anyone else who can do it. Damn that bastard boy, he'll be the death of her yet." Lylie could feel the force of Po's shame flooding from him across the camp and couldn't meet his eyes. What was there left to say?

Raising desperate eyes Pitter's voice softened, "Can you do something, Lylie, can you bring her back to me, we … I, I need her back, I can't watch this no more. I ain't got … she's gonna need to fend for herself, maid, do you understand now?" Tears rolled down his weathered cheeks and he stuttered to an anguished stop.

Lylie looked away from him, her mind whirling. When would Rina be back, she didn't think it would be for a while.

Her eyes fluttered across to the wicker crib laid in the shade of the old oak, just a few feet away, a sleeping Rose quiet within.

"Lylie," a warning growl from the other side of the camp, carried suddenly and clearly on the breeze. "Rina's coming, you *must* wait." Po strode into her line of vision, eyes narrowed. "Tommo's on his way; wait Lylie, wait for them." His tone was urgent, imploring. Pitter turned to him aggressively, "Leave her, Po, you owe us this, all of you do," and he turned accusing eyes around the camp, encompassing the silent figures surrounding them, "She knows she is bound to help; she's got no choice."

"It wasn't her, you fool," hissed Po through gritted teeth, his face grey, "you know it wasn't anyone but Daniel." His voice grated on his son's name; "It was Daniel," he continued, "and the boy has paid. He's paid for many a year." In a conciliatory tone he went on, "We're all sorrier than you'll ever know, Pitter, every one of us, but it's done and can't be undone, leave us be man. Take the maid home where she belongs."

Pitter stood a moment locked in a ferocious stare with Po, before drawing his clenched hands from his pockets and unfurling his fists. "I'll go nowhere, Po, not until she," and he jerked his grey head towards Lylie, "does what she can and," he looked back into Lylie's eyes, "she can, and we both know it."

Po stood staring at Pitter, holding his gaze. The camp was still and silent, hardly daring to breathe, the air heavy and oppressive. The noiseless rooks watched on, as the river waited, its usual chatter dampened and submissive.

Lylie looked up suddenly, straining her head to one side; "Tommy," she murmured to herself, the relief evident on her face. A low moan broke from Pitter's lips, "Lylie, please," he begged, "help me, we bin friends this many a long year, help me, maid, for the sake of my gal." His lips trembled as he gulped down his emotion, he knew full well that Tommo wouldn't be so easy to sway. "Lylie, she's my only child, please, I can't abide this no longer."

Lylie rose unsteadily and as her lips parted to speak a strong voice broke the expectant silence as Tommo strode urgently into the camp, "Lylie, stay yourself darling, we'll talk tonight. Now's not the time, the maid's just waking." Lylie turned her head slowly to the cot, where the blankets moved gently, and with a deep sigh she turned to Pitter. "I'll do what I can," she said quietly and as Tommo attempted to break the flow of her words, she held up her hand stopping him abruptly. "Tommy, he's right though, isn't he? We stand as one, every single Romany here. All of us owe this man." Raising her head proudly she closed her eyes and willed her daughter back. Time was scarce now and looking into the worried faces around her, she turned unsteadily to walk past her stirring daughter and make her way to the churchyard and her Mam.

The heart fire blazed as Po stacked the dried wood below the kettle, his profile stern. He was suffering again, Lylie could tell, it would never go away, what Daniel had done would stay with him for ever. The boy had blighted more than his own life, much, much more. The others tiptoed around Po, afraid of the anger he held in check, worried that he would relapse into the withdrawn and wounded man he had been for so many years previously.

Evening came earlier than she wanted and the meal they prepared tasted like sawdust in her dry mouth. Still, she waited, but she was afraid, afraid that her guilt in the situation would force her hand.

Rina was due back shortly, but her frantic efforts to get home quickly seemed thwarted at every step. She heard her Mam's call, and with every uneven and agitated breath she took she knew that her Mam was in terrible danger.

She had taken her herbs and tonics to the market in the next town over, and although she had managed to get a lift there with a local farmer, she had to walk some of the way back before she managed a ride with the village shopkeeper. It was taking an age and the anxiety was killing her.

Her heart was in her mouth, she prayed her Mam wouldn't start anything without her, she had the Pendant around her neck, the thought of her Mam trying to heal this wrong without the aid of the Pendant was unthinkable. *And with the Pendant?* She asked herself, and yet again, chillingly, the answer was probably, *'unthinkable'*.

Lylie watched and waited, her lips silently mouthing the charms and enchantments of the Guardians. Watching closely, she thought she could detect the merest slackening of the girl's unyielding limbs.

It felt like hours had passed since Lylie started the cleanse that she recognised would bring her no good. She knew that her power alone would hardly be enough to fight the girl's demons, but if it at least made the maid easier until Rina got back, then she would continue with the Pendant. The Others sat around them, the heart fire glowing, their linked hands uniting them in their task, boosting the protection, she didn't feel quite so alone, knowing they were all there for her.

Abruptly Lylie exhaled loudly, fiercely, as she felt a sudden surge of darkness rush into her body, liquid and angry, its furious tendrils reaching deep into her mind, grasping and leeching. A dark destructive hunger raised its head within her, and belatedly, agonisingly, she recognised she wasn't nearly strong enough for this battle, and she was afraid, more afraid than she had ever been.

For an instant she saw the girl's eyes shift to her quickly, showing a depth of despair and loss that left her reeling, and then the moment was gone as her face loosened back into blankness.

Lylie rose unsteadily to her feet with the last of her strength, her legs almost too weak to hold her, and reaching into the very depths of her mind she spoke to Rina: *help me my babe, the darkness is in me, I can't fight it.*

From a long, long, way away, through the roar of what sounded like the ocean in a furious storm, she could hear the distraught shouts of Tommy as he ran towards her, the roar of fury from Po, and her last coherent thought as she fell into a black pit of desolation, was of her Mam's voice saying urgently, "Hold on my babe, my chavvi, you'll be safe, don't let go, hold on tight."

Kneeling in the dirt beside the track just a short distance from camp, the damp air pressing against her face, Rina, heart pounding, took the Pendant from the neck of her dress with trembling hands; she couldn't make it back in time. She could catch her Mam's stream, and it was killing her.

She couldn't make it back in time, dear God, help me, help me, please, … …oh Mam.

Raising the Pendant high before her, her arms outstretched, her body rigid with fear, she cried out frantically, brokenly, for only the second time in her young life:

'*Elders I call to thee, Materfamilias, Seraphs, Old Souls and Guardians approach our table, share our fire, for tonight we request your guidance. We beg you wake from your otherworldly sleep and grace us with your presence, allow us your instruction, for we find ourselves in dire need of your aid. Come wake, rise, sit with your people, lend us your counsel, we the Romanies call to you………*'

"We answer your call our family."

Chapter 23 – 1959 – Lylie

It had been a long time since the sunlight had reached through the layers of her skin, enough to warm her at any rate. If she could have been bothered, she would have wondered why, but she hadn't been bothered. It had been an endless autumn of sorrow, the leaves falling as though lifeless bodies were cascading down around her, and her booted feet had walked over them, crushing them to dust, indifferently.

Rose was walking now, unsteady on her toddler legs, and for a long while now had kept her distance from the stranger who looked like her Mam, but didn't play, or hold her against her body absorbing her baby smell, or bathe and feed her.

This stranger no longer reached for Tommy on cold nights, or laughed quietly at his stories, or smoothed his bronzed cheek. This stranger turned from him; her body cold.

They had lost her, but she was there all the same. There had been so many days when they wondered if she would ever find her way back to them, whether the stairs to the light were too steep for her to climb. Whether, in fact there were any stairs at all, or perhaps it was just an endless dark corridor with no escape?

The despair had touched them all and the camp became a morose and gloomy parody of what it had once been, each Romany feeling the loss of one of their own very deeply. Every Romany united in their grief, humbled in the helplessness of watching the suffering of Lylie's family day in day out, while Lylie sat in solitary agony, inaccessible to them all, locked in her solitary hell.

Rina had been bereft, the guardians had come at her call, they had done what they could; they had saved Lylie's life, dragged her back using all their otherworldly wiles to tether her to her body, until they themselves were exhausted of power, vanishing weakly into the night, Gram disappearing last of all, broken and despairing, but Lylie had already been consumed with the darkness that the gal had carried within her for more than a decade.

"Rina?" he approached her tentatively, his voice such a question, that she had to look up at him, even though her spirits were so low that she had no energy left. Her days were spent caring for her Mam, Rose and Tommy, who although fighting his devastating grief every minute, was a shell of his former self. His strength and his very bearing were so diminished by the loss of Lylie, he hardly looked to be the same proud man he used to be; he appeared a shadow of himself.

"Rina?" Po repeated, and she dragged herself from her thoughts, to see him standing before her, serious and intent. "Po?" she questioned back vaguely, quietly, "What is it?" Her voice held not an iota of interest and the loss of her vibrancy, her life force, made Po desolate. He loved her like a daughter, *please God let her listen to him.* "I need to talk to you, maid, it's important, something you need to hear. A plan, well a sort of idea, I need to run past you." She continued the peeling of the vegetables for the evening meal, but raised her head enough to say disinterestedly, "Ok, go on then, Po."

"No," he said abruptly, more sharply than he'd intended, "not here, no one else should hear, not until we've talked it through, maid." She looked up at him and finding a small spark of interest growing, caused by his abrupt manner, quickly stifled it, what was the point?

Sighing she placed the peelings at her feet, and standing up and brushing herself down, said, "Let's go to the river then, I could do with stretching my legs. Dad, look out for Rose, I'm away for a minute.". Tommy raised his empty eyes briefly and nodded unsmilingly as he turned towards the toddler who was squatting next to his chair, clutching a small doll, and chatting to herself. Rina allowed herself a quick glimpse of Lylie as she sat alone under the oak tree, dry eyed and silent, gazing into the distance.

Rina's thoughts were consumed with that night; the night that took her Mam from them. What she should have done differently, why she shouldn't have gone out hawking, why she hadn't caught Mam's stream earlier… day and night the questions overwhelmed, chipping away at her relentlessly.

Bitterly she remembered old man Pitter walking from the camp that evening, his daughter vague and disorientated, moving alongside him, but no longer the walking dead that she had been earlier in the day.

She could read the old man's thoughts as clear as day as he led his daughter away quickly, escaping the torment and turmoil that they left in their wake. Pitter's stream caught her straight in the chest like a mallet; "*Your turn now, yours, you hear me, you did this, you bastard Romanies, and now it's your turn, your turn to suffer and it's bin too long comin' so go to the hell we bin at this last 10 year, you heathen bastards.*"

Although Gram had been with them when the Guardians rose, her only desperately sad advice had been: '*bide your time my chavvi, my babe, time will out*'. But time *had* passed, and Lylie was worse, she was sinking slowly, drowning in the foul, fetid darkness, and they could reach her less and less.

Rina knew that time was running out, Lylie had been gone way too long.

Po led her to the bank of the river, and they settled themselves on a log careless of the damp of the old wood. The river chattered excitedly. Rina was here, she'd been missed for such a long time and the water welcomed her back like a frenzied puppy. She turned for a moment to stare into its tumbling, chattering flow and smiled a subdued greeting, *'Hello friend. And you,'* she sent soundlessly, raising her eyes to the rooks above her. They regarded her silently, their beady eyes glimmering, offering regal nods of their satin heads in acknowledgement.

Po, cleared his throat, warily, was it wrong to raise the maid's hopes? He asked himself yet again the same question that reared its irritable head, night after night. Maybe it was better to let it go … but *what if, Po*, the voice whispered: *what if?* His mind swirled with the relentlessness of the quandary, but he was here now, and she, Rina, well God knows, he wanted her back too, they all did, they needed her, but it seemed she'd upped and left the same time as her Mam. He sighed deeply, if there was a shadow of a chance, for dear Lylie, for his precious Rina, then shouldn't they try, at least try?

"Maid listen to me, I bin thinking 'bout things a fair bit." Did he have her attention, her eyes were pinned to her boots, was she listening? "Maid, hear me!" His voice rose in exasperation, and he knew he had to reach beyond her lethargy, time was not on their side.

"Rina," he bellowed harshly, the rooks raising wary heads, "listen to me maid, hiding away like a chavvi won't solve this, stop being a yeller belly." He deliberately goaded her, knowing full well she was anything but. As she turned unbelieving eyes to his, reproachfully, he knew it wasn't enough, not yet. "I'm sick of this self-pity. You. Are. Our. Matriarch. Start acting like it, rouse yourself for the love of God, you're not the only one to lose someone you love." That should do it he thought half shamefully, half impatiently.

"Po!" she gasped in wounded outrage, "how could you? You know full well I'm doing the best I can coping with Dad and Rose and Mam. You must know that! Why are you being like this, what's wrong with you?"

He raised his hand, stopping the flow of her words, "I'm sorry, but, maid, I needed to get you to listen. I have something, I *may* have something, something that could, *might*," he amended quickly, "help your Mam, but I need you to stir yourself, we don't have much time. Lylie's losing her fight. We must act now, gal, you have to listen to me and take heed, do you hear me now?" "Yes, Po, yes I hear you," her eyes held his speculatively, the merest glimmer of hope lingering in their blue depths. "Tell me Po," she whispered, "I'm listening."

"Look, maid, the Pendant was used badly by Daniel all those years ago to do wrong, and then, as was always the case, that ill deed had a reckoning."

Po met her eyes squarely, burying the pain this was causing him; this time he noted, she was listening intently. "We both knows that the Pendant can only ever be used for good; else the consequences are terrible, right?" She nodded at him, her blue eyes searching his fixedly; "Ifen, the Pendant gets used for ill deeds," he continued slowly "we knows it will backfire on him that does it, right? Daniel, well he got put away, and that maid …" and he sighed deeply rasping his hand across the stubble on his face. "Well, seems like both Daniel and the poor maid got the rough end of the stick, it don't seem fair on the maid, my gal, but that's how I bin picturing it worked out."

"Now..." he shifted stiffly on the damp log, "it seems to me, that Lylie has took the brunt of the maid's share of that curse. Your Mam never knew the curse had to go somewhere else, and ifen it weren't settled on that maid, where else do you think it would go?"

Rina inhaled a slow, horrified breath, "Oh Mam." She drew a shuddering lungful of air; "Mam took the curse? Mam lifted it from that poor maid and now she's got it? Oh, dear God, do you think that's what wrong with her? Oh Po", she wailed brokenly, "what ...."

"Stop maid," he barked, his eyes hard, "we aint got time for that now." "Listen to me, what if we," he continued, "well you, my chavvi, what if you, asked the Pendant to redirect that curse Lylie's bin hostin', what if the Pendant could take it and put it somewhere else? I'm saying, maid, what if another body took the curse instead of your Mam?"

While he paused briefly. Rina jumped from the log, almost falling in her haste: "No!" she cried frantically, "No Po, I won't let it have you, I won't I can't. There must be another way, I can't lose you too, Po." Reaching out she grabbed at his waistcoat, pulling him to her as tears streamed down her face, and broken sobs tore from her body.

"Maid, maid, stop now." Pulling her hands from him, he stepped back from her grasp and lifted her head to look into her hollow eyes and said agonisingly, "It aint me I was thinking of, my gal, *dear God forgive me*, it aint me."

Chapter 24 – 1959 – The Curse

He stood at the back, far from the edge of the camp, his eyes squinting into the early evening light. The warmth of the day had nearly passed and he felt stiff from lying in the grass, staring all day at the camp. The Romany heart fire, once his friend and comfort, smouldered gently sending up a spiral of apple wood smoke in the distance.

The chavvies were bent over a tin cup with little twigs, stirring some make-believe concoction, their dark heads touching, chatting and laughing.

He could smell his own body, the fear and the anger lingering on his breath, the reek of bitterness rising from him, surrounding him in the hostile odour of discontent. His fists clenched involuntarily; open and shut, open and shut, over and over again, while shallow, terse breaths issued from between his sore lips. He pushed his unkempt hair behind his ear impatiently, hating how unclean it felt.

He was afraid, aching and afraid, but most of all he was angry, and his anger fed him, kept him alive with its strength of purpose.

He'd watched them all, he'd been watching for months now, lying low at the far side of the river, listening to the water chastening him, one instant persuasive, the next angry, cajoling one moment, remonstrating the next. Even that bloody river is on their side he'd thought maliciously. He threw his cigarette butt over his shoulder into the water, and waited while the river grumbled and hissed its annoyance.

He'd smiled at the restlessness he knew he caused; the atmosphere he created within the camp. They knew he was there, each and every one of them, the narrow-minded bastards, but they let him be, the sodding cowards. He lay on his back staring into the blue of the sky, where small clouds floated by peacefully, an endless mystery of nature.

They always thought they were better than everyone else with their damned stupid Romany beliefs; the ridiculous faith that virtue held the stronger hand. He sniffed, well, he'd show them different, he smiled derisively, his dry lips curling painfully with the mocking gesture; how he scorned their faith and unity, their trust and belief in one another. He mocked, *yes mocked*, their very culture and race. Why had he been born into this incestuous bunch of bloody hypocrites, why, oh why the bloody hell couldn't he have been born a Gorja?

He'd watched from afar, with deep satisfaction, Lylie, Pitter and the maid. Bye she weren't a looker, he'd smirked bitterly, he couldn't think whatever he seen in her, even for that brief moment. The years hadn't been kind, oh no, she didn't have a thing about her. Still needs must, maybe he'd visit her again, he should have enough strength for one last go at her, that should get them talking, probably see old Pitter off too by the looks of him. He chuckled maliciously to himself.

The night of the guardians, now that was a sight to behold; he'd watched as they surrounded Lylie, keening their love and support, wrapping her in a pulsing, rippling light, attempting to drag the darkness from her body. He watched and revelled in their distress, the anguish they had carried away with them, when they had done all they could do, and yet, it was still not enough.

He'd seen Lylie's Mam, Old Gram, trailing behind them, her luminous arms still reaching desperately for her child, whilst the strength to remain drained from her. God, he'd relished that moment. And look at Lylie now, served her right, she, and all of them, they should have stood by him, he'd been one of them for Christ's sake, he was *family*.

Rina, the little bitch, she'd set off that morning, going hawking he suspected, and he'd half wondered if that would have been the time to act, but he was glad he'd waited. He'd make this a physical battle this time, he'd show his hand, but only when it was too late for them all.

Last time they'd called up the Guardians, he remembered feverishly, he'd been banished from the outskirts of the camp. The buggers had displaced him, forced him away, he'd left his meagre belongings, all his worldly goods, on the side of the river, as they manhandled him, their forms ethereal and wispy, yet strong enough to guide with force, a full-grown man from the site. Oh, and keep him away with their hexes. But not for ever, no, that power had worn off, he was free, and he was back.

Lylie had the babe now, and she was done for anyway, not in her right mind. Now was a good time; Tommo was a half man; Po, his Father, well he could take him. But first he'd burn the others out.

He needed that Pendant though, what good was he without it? Without it he was useless, but without it, so were they. What power he would have then, the world would be at his beck and call, and why shouldn't he have it? He was one of 'them' after all, he had as much right.

Since the night the Guardians rose, and Lylie had been taken ill, there had been no more hawking, no chavvies playing, no Romanies laughing around the fire at night. There had been no laughter at all, they were destroyed, and as much as Daniel wanted and needed to get in to the camp to steal the Pendant, or set the fire, no one ever went anywhere or did anything to allow him a chance to.

Months had passed, Lylie sat like a statue under the oak tree, while Rina and Tommo crept around like wraiths, doing the chores, preparing meals and waiting on her. The baby had no Mam it seemed, because she never picked the little gal up, not once in all the months he'd been watching.

Occasionally his Father would look over, staring him right in the eye, but Daniel knew Po couldn't see him; maybe he could sense him there? But he never came near, not that Daniel wanted him to, the days of Father/Son were long gone.

With the evening sun warming his back he stared into the camp. Rina was there with the old bastard Po? Pa? Dad? what a laugh, calls himself a Father, the first chance he'd got he'd turned him in to the Gavvers. What sort of a Father turns his own son in? So much for blood being thicker than water, blood ties my arse. His heart was racing with his temper, his vitriol, and he deliberately slowed his breathing, *pace yourself man,* he muttered fiercely, *or you'll snuff it before the job's done.*

He watched with acrid bitterness, Po, leading Rina to the river, chatting to her like he never had with him. She'd even reached out and hugged his Father, *his Father*, the needy bitch, clinging to him tightly, and Po had looked down at her with the love which should have been his, with pride and admiration, and with respect. Daniel felt such a hate billow within him, he could hardly contain it.

But he didn't have enough strength to waste any more of it on them. His body wasn't healthy enough for all the spite he carried, soon, very soon he'd make them pay. Once he got that Pendant, by God, they'd pay. With a half-smile of satisfaction on his cracked lips, he tilted his head curiously as an unusual noise reached him.

Turning his body, he looked back towards the river, and squinting through the late afternoon sunlight, he could see birds lining the bank along the river's edge, as the water furled restlessly, froth peaked waves rising and dipping erratically. A chilly breeze caught at him a moment later, making him shiver and the hairs on his arms stand up. He wondered when he had last eaten or drunk anything; time for a fire and a whisky, it was getting colder.

As Daniel's thin body rose from his view point, he noticed the cloud at the other side of the water's edge farthest from him. The mass was long, several feet in fact, rising almost as much in height. It reflected chaotically in the turbulent surface of the river, a grey mass of eddying movement, twisting and swirling as it made its way across the top of the water, moving solidly and menacingly. As it approached Daniel felt a twinge, he thought it might be fear, something he had so rarely felt, he hardly recognised what the feeling was. He shrugged, *whatever*.

Halting in his movement towards his makeshift camp, he glanced into the clouds depths and thought he could see birds. Rooks? Flying effortlessly within the core. They looked like specks of poison in a thick murky soup, and he sniggered at his flight of fancy, yet still the mass came, and another part of him wondered lazily what it would feel like to breathe in that murk, would it taste of anything?

He bent nonchalantly, brazenly almost, to pick up some kindling, just as the edge of the grey murk reached him. It tasted like death he thought, amazed at his strange knowledge. He recoiled sharply, when the fear started to explore him, entering through his nose and mouth with each anxious breath he took. The terror was consuming him; he felt heavy with dread, a horror and an anguish, so immense, that he knew his fragile body could not survive it.

The water roared ominously in his ears, as suddenly, the rooks flew from the centre of the mass, raging at him, clawing and tearing at his meagre flesh, until he staggered, doubled over in his efforts to escape the onslaught, towards the river, where branches of water, surging feet high, claws of water, solid with the force of intent, reached for him viciously.

He felt his body lifted roughly; and gagging and retching convulsively he frantically attempted to eject the water from his lungs. But the river was relentless, filling his mouth mercilessly with its life force, filling his lungs to bursting point with pressure. He tried desperately to cry out, gasping and retching uselessly, and just before he was dragged, like a ragdoll, into the waiting depths of the turbulent mass, he managed to gasp out hoarsely with his last bubbling, water filled breath: "Run .... run, get 'way, don't let ...."

The Romanies watched with trepidation and some curiosity, the cloud mass rising from beyond the river bank, the chavvies racing towards their parents, clinging to them while the adults muttered gentle comforting words.

The heart fire held it course, fluttering pleasantly, unperturbed by the unfolding events. When the chill wind brought the others closer to its flame, it welcomed them and bade them rest and they drew comfort. They watched and waited silently, as Po and Rina walked towards them from the river bank, united in their steps, heads high and proud, in no hurry. It'd been a fair time since Rina stood as tall.

Tommo stood silently; Rose clasped in his arms. He had little interest in the events unfolding before him, not while Lylie still sat vacantly, staring into the distance, beneath the oak, alone and suffering, fighting with demons, holding on for now. And he clenched his eyes shut tightly against the images he raised.

The others stood watching the mass; they stood in a united silence seeing the scene unfold, waiting for whatever would be, to be.

When finally, the mass had risen and dissipated, when the rooks had turned to roost, Rina took Po's hand turning him away gently from the scene before them, feeling the uncontrollable trembling, the weakness of grief and loss, and she led him to his van like a child, pausing only long enough to pick up the kettle from the fire.

The others parted for them, their eyes holding a deep sadness for the Watcher, they couldn't comprehend what had happened, but they knew that yet again, it seemed it hadn't been good for Po. They reached for him as he passed them by, comforting him with their hands, stroking his back, murmuring gentle words of love in the old tongue.

She braced him as he made his way inside, stumbling, his legs barely strong enough to support him, and taking the rug from the bed, she sat him down and wrapped it around his shaking shoulders. "Po," she whispered through the tears that coursed down her cheeks. "Po, he was in torment, Daniel, he wasn't right; you did what was best for us and for him, he'll rest now, do you hear me, Daniel's at rest now." Shaking his head, unaware of her presence even, he stared at the floor, his turn to be lost to them all.

She didn't know if maybe all she'd done was lose another person she loved, whether Po would be strong enough to come back from this, and pressing the cup of tea into his hand, bending his fingers around the warmth of the tin, she'd turned bleakly to leave him, her heart heavier even, than it had been before. She looked back at his lonely, grief-stricken form, only he could process this, and he needed time, please God let there be enough time.

She turned from closing the van door gently, and stoking his old dog's greying head, instinctively raising her eyes, gazing across the silent camp.

They stood, their Romany bodies turned as one, watching another scene unfold, but this time it was welcome, and their breaths were locked in excited expectation.

"Tommo," Lylie said; and he jerked backwards shocked and startled, his dark eyes wide and incredulous, not daring to believe. She reached with a trembling hand to smooth his bronzed cheek, running her fingers gently down his face in wonder. "I'm back my darlin', my Tommy," she whispered gently as she drew back. And looking deep into his eyes said, "I'm back, my darlin' man, and I'm never going to leave you again."

She reached for Rose taking the mesmerised child from his paralysed arms, and turning, looked across the heads of the others, and straight into Rina's eyes "You did good my babe, my gal." Holding her Mam's gaze, Rina nodded her eyes shining brightly, her body suddenly taller, straighter, her heart filling up. "Mam," she whispered. "Sshhh, maid, there's all the time in the world for us, but Po needs me right now."

Chapter 25 – 1978 – The Hollow

Mum paused in her story telling, catching her breath and Dad started to rustle about, getting the cookies out of the bag, unscrewing the thermos while fending off Libby, who had decided to give up being the 'sensitive' child and tripped Elsie over in the race to get the next biscuit; still, she won, and her small face triumphant and mischievous, turned to Elsie as she spluttered gleefully through a mouthful of crumbs: "Yummeeeee, it's buuutiiiiful I'm eating *all* of them." Screams of outrage ensued, with Elsie hurling herself into Mum's lap to grab the cookies for herself, and subsequently scattering them all over the floor of the hollow.

After we'd all calmed the girls down, and finished huffing sternly whilst giggling secretly, at their performance, I looked across the now quiet hollow to Binny. She sat, her back against a tree, gazing into the brambly wall of foliage which was hiding us from the outside world.

Her eyes were unfocussed, wide, and so still, not even blinking, it looked like she was sleeping, awake, her raven hair dull.

For a moment I thought to leave her, to give her a moment of peace, God knows she'd been through enough with this family, she was probably on overload, but Jon's hand brushed my arm, and turning to look at him, I saw his worried eyes, heard him mouth quietly, "Something's up, go talk to her."

I stood quietly, brushing the dry earth from my trousers ready to go to over, but suddenly, she turned vacant, unblinking eyes in my direction. Her mouth moved but no sound came out to begin with, and a feeling of dread started to wend its way up my arms. I was frozen in place.

She spoke abruptly, eerily calm, and it stopped the conversation between Mum and Dad, halted the girls in their bickering, and I heard Jon's breath draw in sharply.

Rather than the news being shocking when she spoke, it was the look of total horror on Binny's face which had us all transfixed, but in contrast, her words were measured and sure:

"My Mother is on her way."

Broken from my brief moment of immobility, I rushed to her, pulling her into a tight hug, rocking her stiff body back and forth like a child, and for a minute or two, the stunned silence in the hollow was unbroken, even the birdsong ceased its cheerful melody.

Dad was beside me in the next instant, his eyes creased in concern. Kneeling down he quickly took Binny's still, cold hands into his own, wrapping them up in his warmth, and looking into her shadowed, bleak eyes, said, "That sounds to me, like you think it's a bad thing, Binny." When she didn't reply, he turned to look back at Mum, "Is it Katarina, is it a bad thing?"

"Samuel, her Mother's not near enough yet, I can't tell until she's closer. I can't see her, my stream doesn't reach that far, unless ...." she looked at him with concern, their eyes locking, *'.... unless I use the Pendant.'*

"The lady comin' soon, and she mad, mad, mad," crooned a small singsong voice into the stillness. Turning, with unease, our eyes found Elsie, sitting cross legged on the ground, beside Mum. Her eyes were shut, her face serene, a picture of calm, as she chanted the words gently into the warm, leaf scented dell. Libby sat beside her, unfazed, munching on another cookie, crumbs clinging to her lips, her blue eyes totally focussed on a small beetle, making its way across the fine, dry soil.

Mum's disconcerted blue eyes met Dad's fearfully, and he settled a quick but reassuring smile on her, saying in a business-like tone, "Now Katarina, come on, she's our child, what do you expect?"

"Oh, Samuel, she's so young for goodness' sake, I can't believe it!" Turning her face away, she tried to stem the flood of emotion that threatened to overwhelm her.

"She won't remember, Mum, it'll all be like a dream, look at her."

Jon nodded his head towards Elsie, who was crawling on her seven-year-old knees over to the cookie bag, that Libby had placed a couple of protective hands over. "Go on, Mum, look," she turned back unwillingly, and gazed at the girls, who were bickering over the biggest cookie, and raised her eyes with a giant effort. "Oh God, *all* of us…...?" she questioned weakly.

We were looking at Mum, not meeting each other's eyes, and that also included Dad, and we were saying nothing, just mulling over the possibility, when a quiet voice behind us, answered Mum unexpectedly, and the words staggered us to our roots. "Yes, Mrs James," Binny said, stiffly, sitting forward and turning towards us, "I'm afraid so, I think you will find that in fact, it *is* actually, all of us."

"Did you always know?" I asked her later when the furore had died down. "What, about me or about you?" she asked back. "Both I guess?" She looked at me hesitantly, "Not really, I suppose no, not really. Well, I knew about me of course, not really about you. But you know what they say, don't you?" I looked at her shrugging my shoulders, "What?" "Well, they say that birds of a feather flock together, and you know, well us and the school and the bus and where we live, I started to think that maybe, well maybe, some things were just meant to be."

She went on, looking down and drawing small circles in the dusty earth with her finger, "And then I thought to myself, why? Why were things meant to be, and then I thought, what if, what if Anna has …. What if she's ….?" She stopped. "Do you know what I mean?" I looked back at her, one of my favourite people. "Yes, I do know what you mean, Binny," and we smiled stupidly at each other.

"Your Mother?" I said, hating myself, as she tightened her lips imperceptibly. I felt my family stiffen as they listened but carried on stoically with their 'pretend conversation' over at the other side of the hollow. "Yes, my Mother," she sighed. "It's a story that I don't really understand, but there is something odd going on." She looked at me, then past me, and raising her voice slightly, called over to them, "Could you …. would it be okay if you all listened for a moment, please, Mr and Mrs James?"

Mum, Dad and Jon, looked up, pretending they hadn't been listening all along.

"Mum found the school, our Convent, Anna." She continued slowly, "She went there, she talked to the Headmistress, and she enrolled me." She looked at us, sitting around her in a circle, even the girls sat still, gazing at her expectantly. I wondered what they thought they would hear, and knowing what I now knew about Elsie, and really, hadn't I always known about Libby, and her kindness, her 'magic touch', the gift of such calm and tenderness that seemed to take away all the angst from your body, well knowing that, they knew enough to be party to this chat, that's for sure.

Binny sighed into the expectant silence, "Mum's not, she's never been, a … well, a Mother, to be honest. She doesn't really seem to *feel* anything." Binny shrugged her shoulders despondently, "She doesn't laugh, or mess around, we don't play games or have girl time together, we don't, you know, we don't ever hug or even say good night before bed. It's always been that way. I never get a gift from her for my birthday, it's always been thought about and bought, even wrapped by Dad. I just thought that's how it was in every family."

We looked at her steadily, not meeting each other's eyes, silent and so very sad for her.

"I suppose you don't miss what you've never had," she said; "or maybe even question it, until, well until you suddenly find out that other Mothers aren't the same." She looked at Mum earnestly, "Until you know how different it can be, or how different it should be."

She paused, and looking almost shamefaced, though why she should, I didn't know, continued, "Do you know, my Mother has never cried, not ever, not when the dog died, not when Dad was in hospital, not even when something really sad comes on the tv. It's like she's a living, walking, cleaning, robot.

"She's quiet, but she's hostile. I would go as far as to say she …" Binny paused and swallowed, "I would go as far as to say, that my Mother doesn't really like me… actually, no, I wouldn't say that, what would I say? I would say ….my Mother dislikes me, not even a little bit, she, she, dislikes me …. rather … intensely."

The silence around us when she finished, was stupendous. Looking at her it felt like she had opened her very soul to us, left herself raw and exposed, and I felt the tears coursing down my face and into my mouth, I was unable to speak.

She'd never once said anything to me, why hadn't I known, at least made the effort to find out? I could've been a much better friend than I had been, I berated myself bitterly. It's always about you Anna, I thought, always you, and she had been suffering in silence all this time. I shook my head, appalled at my selfishness and self-absorption.

"Your Mummy is sad," came a little voice intruding into my shame, and Libby, scooting carefully across the dirt on her pyjama clad bottom, reached up a grimy hand to touch Binny's face gently, and wipe away a stray tear that had sneaked down her cheek.

"She needs a big hug and girl time to make her all better and when she comes, *I* will hug her, a great big hug until she stops being sad. Then she will feel all lovely, Binny."

We looked at Libby with her shining eyes, you could feel the love flowing from her in waves. Binny gazed deeply into her eyes and taking her hand, kissed it gently. "Do you know Libby; I think you could fix my Mother. If anyone could, you probably could."

"I *can* fix her Binny, *I can, I can*, and she will hug *you* lots too."

"She's here," came a singsong chant from Elsie, "and she not sad, she's mad, mad m…." "Enough Elsie," barked Dad, a little sharply, bringing her back to us with a look of confusion on her face, and earning himself a narrow-eyed look from Mum.

"Samuel will go and meet her, won't you, Samuel?" came Mum's brisk order as Dad turned away a little shame-faced, towards the almost impenetrable foliage. "Me coming too, Dad," Libby raised herself swiftly from the ground, and took his hand forcefully, brooking no arguments. "I come and hug Binny's Mummy, til she isn't S.A.D," she spelt out over her shoulder to Elsie who looked back at her, tilting her head brazenly and mouthing M.A.D gleefully.

"Don't bring her here, Samuel," Mum shook her head at him emphatically, "not here, okay?" "Of course, not darling, of course not, don't worry. We'll be back soon, just stay calm; I'll think of something." His face creased in worry, "She's going to want to see Binny though." He turned to her, "Binny, darling, do you think you should come too?" Looking up at him, she burst out tragically, "Oh no Mr James, please no, I can't, really I can't, please don't make me!"

"Right, of course, yes, well we'll go and sort things then," and he looked at Mum his brow furrowed in concern. "It's ok, Samuel, I'll come too. Anna, Jon, look after Binny and Elsie, we'll be back soon."

Chapter 26 – 1978 – Mauve

Her eyes drilled into them as they stood in the silent dining room of River Meadow Cottage, first Samuel, holding him in a hawk's glare, thin lipped, narrow eyed, before moving swiftly to Katarina. Her eyes lingered finally, on Libby, unreadable, but no real change, she looked devoid of all emotion, but not however, of focus.

"Where is she?" Mrs Binnley said flatly, her lips hardly moving, her tone still indifferent, "her Father said she was staying with you for a couple of days, but…." She stopped briefly, seemingly searching for a semi- courteous way to point out our perceived lack communication with her. "I haven't had a chance to check with you, that Caitlin is not, *'putting upon you'* and *'outstaying her welcome'*. I rather feel I should have checked with you first, before my husband agreed to a *lengthier* stay."

"First of all, let me welcome you to our home, I hope you are well?" Katarina responded stiffly, her very words showcasing the other woman's lack of courtesy, her blue eyes flashing with the hint of a challenge. "I do hope you haven't been worried, Mrs Binnley, we spoke with your husband, and mentioned we would love Bi…, err *Caitlin* to spend some time with Anna. I must admit we *had* presumed your husband had spoken to you and we had your *full* agreement? If not, I can't imagine how worried you must have been, and how sorry we are to have caused you any concern."

Samuel slid his eyes over to her surreptitiously, a half-smile playing on his lips; he enjoyed seeing his wife endeavouring to keep her temper in check, especially after what Binny had told them. As she glanced back at him coolly, he realised that he had been caught out, and he hastily turned his gaze back to Binny's Mother.

"My husband may have been a little vague in terms of the length of Caitlin's stay here," she was saying "and perhaps it would be better if she came home with me. After all, she has several … things … to attend to, and her piano practice is well overdue. We mustn't neglect practice, must we?" A perfunctory smile touched her lips briefly, as she turned her gaze to the meadow behind River Meadow Cottage. "Is Caitlin on her way? I really don't have much time, I have so much to do …"

As Katarina and Samuel raised their eyebrows questioningly at each other, completely lost on how to proceed, a small voice chipped in happily, "No Binny's muvver, she's not coming to see you, she wants to stay with us. She loves us, and she said she doesn't want to go home."

Samuel closed his eyes momentarily at a loss for words, as Libby launched into, "She said you were 'motionless and didn't buy her any presents and you didn't cry at sad stuff on the tele, not ever. She said you wasn't a proper …."

"Libby, that's enough," Katarina cut in sharply, shaking her head in disbelief. That *child*, she thought wearily and raising her eyes looked into the other woman's gaze, she was almost astonished that some form of emotion had played its way across her face. It did appear however that the woman was also struggling with speech, as her lips moved, but no actual sounds escaped her.

Katarina and Samuel froze in the midst of frantically trying to conjure up some solution to the awful situation, when to their, what could almost be described as horror, Libby walked towards Mrs Binnley and reached for her hand. "Come on Binny's muvver, don't be sad, my Mummy will teach you to be a really good Mummy and then Binny will love all your bones." She smiled up beatifically at the speechless woman, and pulling her along the lawn by the edge of her coat, she said with all the excitement of a five-year-old, "We can sit by the river and I will fix you, then Mummy will learn you, all her lovely Mummy stuff."

The breeze eddied around the chestnut trees as they sat on the bank together, the leaves dancing, creating freckles of light on the shaded earth beneath. She'd unwillingly swept her skirt beneath her, seeing no real way out of the farce she deeply regretted she had become part of, that her *blessed* daughter had dragged her into, and glancing around suspiciously, lowered herself on to the soft green meadow grass edging the river. Her knees were tightly clamped together, and her arms hugged them, white knuckled fingers woven together steadying herself in such an unfamiliar position, but for Libby, sitting beside her, the sun glancing off her blonde hair, it was as natural as breathing.

The water burbled and bubbled, its clear depths sparkling as the weed was dragged teasingly by the swift current, and as the sun caught the water, a calmness suddenly reached the woman, its tentative fingers smoothing and caressing. She noticed her breathing steadying and the knots in her stomach easing just slightly.

Feeling a warmth steal onto her hand, she looked down, catching her breath in surprise; a small hand rested gently on the cold, white skin, a sun kissed golden hand, the hand of the child.

Gasping, almost in pain, she frantically raised her eyes. The unfamiliar feelings of love and contentment infiltrating her restraint, breaking her guards, were frightening and uncontainable; she didn't know where to put them, where they fitted into her body, how she could store them, how she could keep them safe and visit them later, alone, *please God.*

The ripples of weed tugging gently back and forth with the flow of the water was mesmerising, the child's hand warm, her voice gentle and rhythmic, singsong with a musical cadence, as she called to the fire, to the water, to the earth, and to the air, seeking their service and their aid.

Her limbs felt leaden as the pulse of the chanting filled her veins, flowing sinuously through her muscles and bones, entrancing every nerve and cell, cleansing and comforting her to the depths of her soul. The soul she hadn't even acknowledged an existence of, for the better part of her adult life.

Sensations came flooding back, the smell of the crushed grass beneath her seated body, the sounds of the water, skipping and dancing merrily as it flowed past, positive in its path. She titled her head, birdlike, almost excited as she listened to the breeze in the leaves of the old chestnut trees, the birds chattering in the leafy depths, animated and absorbed in their busy world. The breeze played around her face, lifting the edges of her hair, teasing the stiff strands into a scruffy halo around her face, as she softened her hitherto, unreceptive features into the unaccustomed lines of a gentle smile.

Her eyes suddenly, unexpectedly brimming, she turned her head to the now still and silent child beside her, and looking down into her blue eyes, breathed, "It's …" and suddenly lost for the words to describe this most enchanting and exhilarating moment, stopped, baffled.

"I know, Binny's Muuver, it is, it's butiful," the child said sweetly.

"I've been … away, so far away," she murmured, "where have I been? I feel like I've been …... Oh …. Oh, dear God, no …no…", she screwed her eyes up in the absolute horror of sudden realisation. *"I think I've ... I've ... oh dear God, what have I done, oh God help me, what have I done?"* She buried her face in her hands, the tears falling from her eyes, moaning and shaking, all the while repeating over and over again, *"Oh dear Lord, what have I done?"*

Shocked beyond belief, Samuel and Katarina looked at each other from their vantage point a few feet away, what on earth had happened? Libby was the healer, the golden child. No one ever came away from a 'moment' with Libby feeling anything but positive, the warmth of the child emanated from her.

But this woman, who only minutes ago had silenced them with her total indifference sat, neat pleated skirt screwed up beneath her, on the riverbank, wailing her sufferings to the four corners of the earth, whilst their youngest child sat beside her, calm and serene, waiting patiently, it seemed, for the pitiless moment to pass.

"Get it out, Binny's muuver, that's it, get it out," she cajoled innocently, sweetly, her voice a mixture of chant and song, "in a minute you will be all fixed, you will see."

"Child," the woman wheezed out almost incoherently, turning to meet her eyes, "but what I've done …. what I've done, you've no idea." She gazed into the young girl's eyes desperately seeking some form of reassurance, anything to hold tight to, something to keep the darkness from snatching her back, desperate for a way to make her actions acceptable. "I can't fix what I've done child. It's too late, oh dear God forgive me, I fear it's much too late."

Chapter 27 – 1978 – The Hollow

"Oh no," Binny's anguished voice whispered, "they're bringing her here," and I knew she was right. The hollow was tense, the leaves stilled their rustling as though the wind too was holding its breath in anticipation. I looked around for Jon and Elsie. They were staring into the thick foliage surrounding the entrance path into the hollow, their eyes wide and disbelieving. What on earth could have possessed them to bring her here?

"Binny," I hissed frantically, "listen to me, tell me now, before she gets in here, how, *how*, did you know about the hollow, about it being our … our, God, you know, our safe place? What made you lead us here; how did you know to?"

She looked back at me swiftly, spilling the words out in her haste to explain before her Mother showed up. "How did *you* know it was your safe place, Anna?" she shot back quickly. "We're the same you and I, you know that, we both know stuff, don't we, we can both do stuff? Look, I was led here, just like you, just like your parents, and your brother and sisters. I'm sorry, but you aren't the only ones you know."

I looked back at her mutely just for a split second as the dense foliage started to part. "Who else?" I whispered urgently, "Who else is like us, Binny?" "Oh Anna," she looked at me sadly, not wanting to be the one to remind me, "Bris, Anna, Bris is like us."

Numb and silent, I sat on the dusty earth, my ears ringing with fear. Of course, hadn't I always known; was it because so far, his actions had been awful, but not necessarily supernatural, that I couldn't recognise that he was the dark side of us? I'd never considered until now, that there was a dark side. Nothing he had done had shown real powers, had it? I thought back to Mum falling into the daisies, *fallen?* I questioned maybe, *maybe not though.* Getting into River Meadow Cottage? Anyone could, couldn't they? Break in and steal?

I remembered back, the coiling sinuous dread, tracing its way through my body, the evil emanating from him. But wasn't that just my fear manifesting itself, my way of dealing with blind terror? Didn't everyone feel like that when they were afraid of someone?

"Do …" I'd gone to ask Binny, but her raised, dread filled eyes had stopped me in my tracks. Her Mother was here.

"Darling," the stranger in front of us, said hesitantly, "would you mind if I sat beside you?" And a reluctant Binny had no choice but to agree. Even so, her face was puzzled, her Mother's demeanour was odd, unlike her usual vacuous look, her face held an unusual blend of something approaching sadness, and other emotions, indecipherable to us.

But this isn't right, I could hear Binny thinking. She gazed stupefied at the woman who settled herself, neat skirt once again bunched up, down on the dry, dusty, earth beside her daughter.

Reaching out a birdlike hand, she took her stupefied, wordless child's hand into her own and said quietly, "I am as sorry as I can ever be, Caitlin, um Binny, my darling. I adore you, you know, you are my daughter, and you are perfect to me."

"Listen," she shuffled closer to Binny, who shrank away from her automatically, "darling, something has gone on, out of my control, but, and I know it's going to take time, but I am here now, and we … we are going to be different together. I …I, am going to be different."

She looked beseechingly at Binny, "Do you hear me, my darling? You have a Mother now, a real Mother, I am her." She smiled tentatively, wistfully, "Please just know, that since before you were born, I have never been me, I don't quite know why, or what happened yet, but believe me, I am going to find out."

Shaking her head, and biting into her lip harshly, she continued on, "But in the meantime, please, please, I beg of you, give me a chance to be something other than the empty vacuous, unapproachable, tyrant, that you have always known. I want to live a life with you full of love and fun and laughter. Please forgive me my darling, I will do everything within my power, to try and be someone you can love. I promise you that."

She looked into Binny's closed face for a second, and sighing said gently, "I don't blame you for guarding yourself from me darling, but I will wait for you, until you're ready. I will wait forever, if that's what it takes. Forever."

The silence encapsulated us all, until at last Binny raised her head and looked into her Mother's eyes, the very merest glimmer of hope in their depths. "Ok", she breathed out finally, "ok, but I will be calling you, Mum, if what you say is true. Mother will be the other person, the one I used to know, that is my rule if we are going to try and move forward. Oh, and one more thing, I … I will be Binny from now on!" She jutted out her chin defiantly; clearly waiting for the first fail of her new Mum. But she didn't have long to wait for her answer; the ecstatic smile of the suddenly vibrant woman beside her, and the joy raised arms, accompanied by a hitherto apparently, according to Binny's indrawn gasp, never heard *whoop*, astonished us all with its abandon. "Yes, yes and yes darling, to everything, God, I love you, Binny, you make me so proud, I, your *Mum*, am so very, very proud."

Jon and I looked at each other, eyebrows raised, before turning back to our tiny miracle of a sister, who stood patient and tranquil, munching on her umpteenth cookie.

"We'll see," said a sceptical, but tremulously hopeful Binny.

Chapter 28 – 1978 – The Pendant

"Forgive us, Mrs Binnley," Dad started, when all the hugs and tears of the morning were finished, for the time being anyway.

"Please," she said, glancing round at all of us, smiling like a child at Christmas, "please, just call me Mauve, I can honestly never thank you enough, and you child," she said gazing fondly at Libby, "you, I thank from the bottom of my heart. Without you, well, what can I say?" Libby gazed back at her calmly, her eyes knowing, "'S ok, Binny's muvver."

Mauve nodded to herself. "I've got a lot of work to do, of course," she glanced at Binny lingeringly, "there's so much I need to say, so much I need to find out, to try and remember, but," her face darkened, "I'm going to try and trace my background, try to get to the bottom of how this could have happened. That's the next step."

She looked at Dad expectantly, "Forgive you, Samuel?" she remembered suddenly. "You were saying, forgive you, why, what on earth for? I owe you so much, surely you realise that?"

"Ah, well," he said reluctantly, "there is a little more that you really need to know." Mum glanced at him raising her eyebrows. "But I ask only one thing of you. Please let us continue from where we left off, time is of the essence, and I do believe that Binny can fill you in at a later stage?" He looked enquiringly at Binny, and she nodded her agreement. "Mum," she said hesitantly, earning a look of happy surprise from Mauve, "Can I tell you about it later? There's so much to explain and … well you're quite a way behind." Grabbing

Binny's hand her Mum said warmly, "Of course, whenever my darling, whenever, maybe over a hot chocolate later?"

Everyone laughed wistfully, and Mauve blushed a trifle, before smiling self-consciously, "There's just so much to catch up on with my girl." Binny caught her gaze with such a look of hopeful contentment, it bought tears to my eyes, *God*, I was so happy for her.

"Right, now…." said Dad, "we are as far forward in our explanation as we have time for, you know enough to realise we need to keep the Pendant safe from Bris. He wants it badly and it seems he'll stop at nothing to get his hands on it. We need a plan."

The hollow had started to darken as the evening set in. "We all know how difficult this will be for Mauve, not knowing the background, but we must keep Binny in the hollow, both for her and our safety, so Mauve will have to stay too. Okay Mauve?" "Samuel, yes," she agreed vigorously, "go ahead, I'll stay silent, there seems to be a problem here that is bigger than my own right now, so, please, do carry on. I'll stay with you all." She earned herself a smile of thanks from Binny, who was trying so hard to believe that her Mum would not convert back to 'Mother' at any given moment.

"Look," Mum began taking over briskly, "we know now that we can't bury or hide the Pendant, it's still traceable. We can't dismantle it." Gasps of dismay at the thought filtered through the hollow, even from the girls. "We cannot destroy it, and I will not agree to that anyway." Dad clasped her hand warmly, his eyes on her. "We cannot drown, burn or melt it. We cannot harm it in other words. However, we can … now listen to me carefully and do not speak yet, please." She held up her hand to ensure silence, catching our eyes, one by one. "We can, I think, I hope …. 'absorb' it. At least, I believe, we can absorb its power. Now if we can," she looked around at us all again, "the actual physical Pendant would be useless, an empty vessel, so to speak, but of course we would keep it and maybe one day, we would be able to reinstate its power.

"Now I've been thinking about this since, well, since Mam was here, that time I had to dig it up when Anna was a baby." She looked across at me and smiled, "You were a nightmare darling, we'd thought to keep you safe, so we buried it, right here in the hollow, but that didn't work. You were so upset, and so was I, of course." She looked into Dad's eyes lingeringly. "So, I dug it up. I came back here, with your Gran and Rose, and I dug it right back up," she smiled to herself, remembering the moment the Pendant was retrieved and was once again resting on her heart. "I've kept it as safe as I can, I wear it always, and up until now, well it's been… untraced." She pulled it from her shirt reverently, and we watched spellbound, as it lay on her chest, glowing and, was it humming?

It was a thing of beauty, ornate and intricately carved, a pulsing golden light flowed from the amber sphere in the centre of the filigree, while the gentle hum caressed the air around them, sweeping away every care in the world. Looking around I saw on our faces, the knowledge that each one of us was in the presence of an ancient and majestic power. The thought of its destruction was unthinkable, unimaginable and terrible.

The silence continued for a few moments after her words, and I felt the need to speak the burning question on all our minds, "Absorb it, Mum, into where, into what, exactly?" She looked back at me, deep into my eyes before answering gently. "Us, darling", she said, "us Anna. I've been thinking, what if we divide the Pendant into equal parts, one part to go into each of us, well actually, you, the four children." She held up her hand and continued swiftly, "And only when you choose freely, and when we come together in full agreement, free of force or manipulation, well then, and only then, would the power in its entirety, once again become the 'Pendant'. Or as Gram would say, God rest her," she looked upwards toward the roof of the leafy hollow, where the dimpsy light, filtered through the tree tops, casting weak shadows on our faces, "as Gram would say … 'The Key'."

A sudden unpleasant noise, a guttural, hoarse gasp, suddenly drew our wide eyes towards its sound. Mauve, seated beside Binny, still holding fast to her hand, was waxen. Sweat lay on her skin causing an unhealthy sheen on her face, and her grasp on Binny's hand appeared, judging by Binny's pained expression, to be tightening perceptibly.

"Ouch Mum, stop, what on earth …" Binny huffed out, but suddenly recognising how distraught her Mum was, stopped and turned to her fully. "Tell me," she asked urgently "tell me what's wrong, Mum, *please*."

The woman appeared frozen into immobility, her eyes pinned to the glowing artifact around Mum's neck, her breathing uneven and distressed. We looked at each other in consternation; *what now?* I know everyone was thinking that we didn't have time for histrionics, we had more important things to do than cater to another crisis, even if she was Binny's 'Mum'.

Visibly steadying herself, she finally spoke, her breath ragged and tortured, "It's the Pendant. I've, I've seen it before, it's hard to remember, but I know I've seen it, and it didn't glow like that, oh no it was, well, it shone, sort of black,

black and … and… oily. It wasn't good, it, oh God it was frightening, awful, no, it was evil … just evil. It wasn't good, it wasn't gold and shiny, oh God…"

"Libby, quickly, go to her," Mum said, "help her, darling. Find out where she was when she saw the Pendant, and who she was with, please, quickly now." Bewildered and upset, we stared at the woman, as she kept muttering unintelligibly, her voice dread filled and terrified.

None of us knew what to do or say, but Libby scrambled to her feet with Mum's help, and pushing past us, plopped down on the ground beside Mauve, prising her clutching fingers, away from Binny's crushed hand.

"Hey Binny's Mum," she chanted softly, "hey, you, it's ok. I will fix it, just like last time, and you will tell me every think, every think you remember from when you seen the Pendant and it was oily, ok now?"

A low moan escaped the woman, and to our horror she fell sideways, toppling heavily against Libby, who shuffled further across the earth on her bottom, to allow the woman to lean on her, displaying no concern whatsoever. "Elsie," Libby called sweetly, "you gonna help me, yes?" Elsie looked far from obliging, but seeing the pain on Binny's face, raised herself slowly and making her way to Libby, half pushed Binny out of the way, and with some irritation, squatted to pick up Mauve's hand to hold it, stroking the skin and closing her eyes, albeit unwillingly. Just before she closed her eyes, I could hear her whisper tetchily, half to herself, ending on a quiet, triumphant note, "M.A.D. I knew it!"

"Daniel, don't, please don't … please," Mauve wheezed aloud, disjointedly, the depth of pain and fear in her voice, almost too much to bear, her eyes screwed themselves tightly shut as the tension left her body in a rush and became suddenly limp; and then, harshly indignant. "I don't want it, it's not mine, get it away, Dad," the voice of a young girl came from Mauve's lips, insolent, but at the same time, curiously devoid of emotion. Low toned and flat voiced, she continued, "It's not mine Dad, I haven't got a baby, get it away from me, he's not mine, he. isn't. mine. Not mine!" Her voice took on a repetitive sing-song drone, "Take it away. I wasn't a bad girl, take-it-away, I wasn't a badgirl, takeitaway, Iwasn'tabadgirl, takeit …." Over and over again until the muttering became incoherent.

Turning my head, at the gasp of horror to the side of me, I was shaken to my core. I saw Jon's eyes follow my gaze and widen in shock. My usually resilient and level-headed Mother was pushing her hand hard into her mouth, to stifle what appeared to be almost silent screams. The noises escaping from her, were truly awful, it sounded as though a wounded animal, was fighting to free itself from her body.

Dad sprang to her side, enveloping her in his arms, crooning to her like a young child. "Hey, hey, Katarina, darling, stop now, stop," ssshing her, and stroking her back, and then finally, firmly, "you're frightening the children, stop Katarina."

But it wasn't over yet.

Broken sobs issued from Mauve's lips and Binny buried her head in her arms, her shoulders shaking. Jon and I scurried to her side, our legs stiff and unwieldly, to crouch and fling our arms around her, not knowing what to say, just holding her to let her know she wasn't alone.

Libby broke contact with the woman, her hand reaching to touch Elsie, and bring her back. "Elsie, come on, it's done now, let's go, get the cookies." They raised themselves absent-mindedly, seemingly unfazed by the situation around them.

Maybe their young minds needed a moment of oblivion, a chance to refresh and process?

"Oh my God, Samuel, oh my God," Mum whispered, devastation written plainly across her face, etched into her features. "Surely, not, it can't be … surely it isn't?" Dad looked back at her, his skin sallow suddenly, his voice halting, but purposeful all the same. "I'm afraid," he said slowly, "that I think it may be. I'm sorry my darling, but things are starting to add up, aren't they? Look, let's just listen for now, don't jump to conclusions until we have all the facts." He looked at her resolutely. "Nothing we do now, Katarina, can change the past, we need to look forward, help her however we can, and …" he wavered slightly, "we have Binny to think of." She drew in her breath in sharply, raggedly; "Dear God, what if he's ……?" "Yes," said Dad grimly, his eyes red rimmed and tired, "what if he is … What *if* Bris is her brother."

The hollow was strained and tense, holding its breath like the rest of us. Into the silence Binny whispered weakly, "Mum? Mum? Are you … are you ok?" Her Mum lay slumped on the dusty ground, tear-stained cheeks mixing with streaks of smeared dirt and the remains of her face powder. The woman who had walked to River Meadow Cottage earlier in the day, could not have been farther from the creature we saw before us now, broken and confused, dirty, unkempt and seemingly isolated in her own memories.

Dear Lord, we looked around at each other, above Binny's bowed and trembling head; all thinking the same thing; our eyes darting from one to the other, panicky and sickened, and thought: *What now? Dear God, whatever now?*

Chapter 29 – The Present – Lorentree Cottage

The fire had died low, and the girls were quiet as I paused for breath. Jon sipped his wine silently, and as the clock struck ten, I heard the wind wail around the eaves of Lorentree Cottage, the sound eery and sinister. Jon turned his head towards me, you better not rest too long, his worried eyes said, once again.

"What had she done?" whispered Elsie. "What had Binny's Mother done? What the hell … and anyway …? Why can't I remember all this, and Libby," turning to our youngest sibling suddenly, she mouthed, almost silently, imploringly, shaking her head in despair, "Libby …?"

Libby sat, still as stone, staring into the fireplace, her face ashen, the wine glass trembling in her hand. "I remember …. Elsie, Anna, I …I … I think I remember."

I looked across at Jon our eyes locking, both of us sending silent messages:

"Now?" "Yes, I think so, don't you? you or me? … Me," he nodded back reluctantly.

Rising from the chair slowly, he walked towards Elsie who, very unlike her usual feisty self, visibly shrank away from him, but crouching down, he lifted her stiff, unwilling hand from the sofa, and rested it between his own hands gently. Elsie raised wild eyes to his; "Shhh," he breathed out softly, "trust me, sis, it's going to be fine, just wait." And raising his head he intoned slowly and clearly, his voice strong:

"I respectfully invite our Guardians to re-establish their connection in this room, around this fire, to your faithful and committed children, namely Elsie and Libby. They have

long been gone from your presence, but we now require your service, should you wish to bless us with your aid."

He bowed his head low, and Lorentree Cottage held its breath in the heavy silence, as the fire roared to life and for just a moment, the clock halted in its persistent ticking.

The flood of emotions on the girls' faces was unstoppable, their features morphing through a catalogue of reactions, changing like the wind, as the urgent tide of a once known consciousness hit them hard, in a welter of lost knowledge.

I could see their minds struggling to come to terms with the overwhelming familiarity of the forgotten memories, the parts of them held hostage, kept undisclosed for so many years.

Oh, I wanted so badly to stop the flood from rising, to keep them safe from what could only be to them, a terrifying overload of lost moments, memories taken without their consent and without their knowledge, but I couldn't do that, we had come this far, it was too late now to back out. Now, they knew too much, and God help us, not yet enough.

God, the guilt was eating me up though, and I could see that Jon, who was still crouching beside the sofa, gazing at the girls, waiting, breath held, was in the same boat.

An age passed, or did it? Time, so the clock showed, held its breath and paused with us, only the fire and the wind and rain outside broke the hush in the room.

It was surprisingly, Elsie, who broke the silence first. I had thought that Libby, halfway to remembering, would have been more likely to regain her composure first, but no, that wasn't the case.

A shift in the atmosphere had Jon suddenly standing, out of harm's way, presumably. I was trying to decide how

I would have reacted to having a huge part of my past just rammed back into my head, memories I had no idea I had lost, and I was guessing that it wouldn't be pretty.

"I feel whole, somehow, isn't that mad?" Elsie said in a bewildered voice. She was hesitant, "It feels as though I've always known, yet I haven't. It should be shocking, I should feel angry I think … but somehow, I just feel relieved, relieved and incredibly whole, as though I'd lost something, and found it again, then thought, oh yes, I remember putting it there." She smiled weakly and said suddenly, more in control, "It's ok, you two, I'm alright." And turning her head asked waveringly, "What about you, Libby? Are you ok, can you remember?"

"Me?" Libby said weakly, her face grey. "Well, let's see: … I'd say I'm shocked, shocked, confused and almost speechless, battered, but not broken, no, not that, but I've got to say," she swept her arms out wide nearly spilling her wine, "this opens up a whole new set of questions, doesn't it now?"

Looking past Elsie towards Jon and me, she said firmly and quite severely for her, "Now I … am going for a rollie, and when I get back in this door, I want to know exactly how we were both eliminated from the enquiry, so to speak, and I want to know by whom, and I want to bloody well know why!"

She stood briskly grabbing her baccy to make her way to the door, nearly jumping out of her skin as Jon barked out sharply, "No! no, sis," and then more kindly, "you can't go out there, absolutely not. There's more going on here than you know, there's real danger, you can't go out." Dropping his voice, he said more calmly, "Smoke in here, by the fire, Anna that's ok, isn't it?" Eyeing him quickly I agreed, "God yes, in here Libby, here is fine, really, really fine."

Looking us both in the eye, she lowered herself slowly back onto the sofa, begrudgingly. "Okay …. in here then, suits me, but for God's sake, you better tell us what's going on out there, we do have to leave at some stage tonight."

I tilted my head suddenly as she lowered her head to shield the match. They were here, I could sense them, so I saw could Jon, and I unfolded my stiff limbs from the armchair and making my way quickly to the door, opened it wide, to usher them inside.

"All done then?" Dad said holding fast to his hat, fresh from the gale outside, the very master of understatement. Mum stood alongside him, white faced, itching to rush to the girls to find out how they were, how the news had affected them, to make sure her babies had survived the revelations of the evening. Her eyes looked them over, searchingly, intently, and they looked back silently, with a mixture of confusion, disbelief and something close to annoyance, fleetingly crossing both their faces.

"Wine, Dad?" Jon asked quietly, breaking the moment, "Mum, you too?"

He rose to go to the kitchen, coming back with two more glasses.

Once their coats were off, and they were scrunched up with the girls on the voluminous old sofa, wine in hand, Dad questioned through a mouthful of brie, "Binny isn't here yet then?" just as a knock sounded at the door. "Yes Dad," I replied evenly, as I got up to open the door, "it seems as though she is."

Chapter 30 – 1951 – The Boy

He watched the boy, a gloomy sort of kid, scuffing his feet around the perimeter of the farmyard, raising the dust, then dragging his boot through the dry earth, grinding his heel into the tinder-like grass over and over again. It was done passively, no real aggression. *Didn't he have chores to be getting on with?* He looked hard, scrutinising the child's face. It held a curious mixture of sullenness and what? *Bravado?* No, no, not that, *grit* … Daniel decided, *grit*, yes, he liked that; *grit* … touched with …. *nervousness? Ha, alrite then,* that could work in his favour, fear was good, fear was his ally, *let's get this done.*

The boy kept casting uneasy glances behind him, towards the house, the others must be there, maybe watching, although he doubted it, the child wouldn't be wasting precious time kicking up dust otherwise. No, Daniel would have to move fast and he'd have to use his own skills, no sodding *Pendant* today.

Rite then; he'd assume the child was *supposed* to be elsewhere, maybe working on the chores that surely came with running a farm of this size, so *decide then Daniel.*

How tall was he? He looked again towards the dark-haired boy, tallish for a twelve-year-old, *was he twelve now*? Yes man, he thought impatiently; *that's how long you bin inside, keep focussed!* So that would mean; *let's see, maybe two, no, say three drops, be careful, he looks light though,* he mulled it over; *two and half then.*

He took the small brown bottle from the inside of his waistcoat pocket and laid it carefully on the grass, reaching to his other side, he drew out a small grubby cloth. Folding it up into quarters he half smiled to himself thinking maybe he was being a bit too considerate, he scowled, a little ashamed, *don't soften now man*, and shaking the cloth free, screwed it into a hard untidy, knot.

Daniel raised his head slowly; his decision made; so *now then, slowly man slowly,* he admonished himself, he's got to just *disappear.*

The boy woke from the deepest of dry mouthed sleeps he'd ever known. Opening his eyes slowly, he tried to focus. It was hard, his head pounded unforgivingly, and for a split second he wondered if he'd knocked himself silly, like he did last year on the yard gate when he pushed it too hard. It had bounced back and struck his head so hard, for a moment everything had gone black. His Gramps in his usual harsh way had just yelled; *get up off your arse boy, we got stuff to do.*

He looked down; he was lying on the grass; his feet and hands bound so tightly he could hardly move his fingers. The bindings looked like old bandages, used, at that, and even he, who only saw the old tin bath on a full moon, felt unclean. "Eyywp," he gurgled, his muffled cry sounding nothing like the word he'd intended, and he'd used the last of his spittle forming it. Ridiculously, considering the predicament he found himself in, he wondered if his mouth would crack and fall to pieces, like the lime plaster on the inside of his Gramp's old barn.

A sudden movement to the side of him caught his eye. A man, dressed in scruffy gypo clothes, sat eyeing him impatiently. His eyes were dark, his skin bronzed and in any other situation, the boy would have aspired to look just like him when he grew up. He was a good-looking man, tall and well built, but something, something in his aura, some awareness of the complete lack of human compassion, made the boy choke hard on his non-existent saliva. A huge swell of fear exploded in his chest as he felt himself shrink further into his own skin in an effort to move himself out of the stranger's stare.

A rusty voice came at him; "I'm your Pa boy. Ha!" Taking in the boy's wide eyes he laughed hoarsely, "Oh, so they didn't tell you 'bout me then?" The smile left his lips. "Did they say I was dead? No?" Reading the boy's eyes, the man continued, "Ah, I see, they didn't tell you that you had a Pa? That rite?" He turned his cheek seeming to sniff the wind, assessing, "Well, you got one boy, I is him. You'm my lad, mine, and from now on, we," and he looked hard into the boy's eyes, his own glittering coldly, "we'se gonna get to know each other. See, I bin waiting a long old time to see you, and your Mam, that stupid, thick, cow ..." he watched the boys eyes widen, "well she never telled me I had a son. Left me hanging she did, I had to be told by a mate. What'd you think of that then?" He looked disturbingly indignant, and the boy watched on with tear filled eyes, straining his hands impotently at the dirty constraints.

"Now, when I can trust you lad, I'm gonna let you out of those binds, but 'til then, you'm gonna be walking the land like a... like a," he screwed up his eyes, searching for the illusive analogy, "like a… Egyptian Mummy," he finished triumphantly. Standing suddenly, his imposing height causing the boy to strain his neck right the way back, said, "Hungry?" The boy nodded back warily. "Rite well let's get on, things to do, places to be." He nodded, pleased with himself, with the job he considered well done. "Otchie for scran tonight, I'll get on it. Me and you boy, we'm a team now. Where I goes, you goes, got it?"

The boy nodded frantically, his stomach twisting with fear. He disliked his Mother that was true, and his Gramps too, come to think of it, but right now he wished with every cell in his skinny, unwanted body, that he was back there, at home, sitting in the kitchen in the morose silence which had so far formed the most part of all of his young life.

"Tether her, damn you, boy," he yelled. Ben nodded back grimly, holding hard to the wayward mare. *Ben!* ... I'm *Ben*, he thought savagely, bloody *Ben*, you cussed old sod. Not hard to pronounce surely? But not once had his Pa, ever, in the years of tramping the land, asked him his real name, not bloody once. *Did he even know it?*

As Ben grew, tall, fit, stronger by the year, Daniel in direct correlation, grew weaker. His once proud bearing was sadly diminished, his hair although still abundant, had grown to an unbecoming, speckled grey. Ben evaluating him, knew deep in his gut that things were not right with the man.

He'd had plenty of opportunities over the years to escape, and at first, he had tried, a number of times. A week after he'd been taken, given a moment to get off the track, for his bladder called to him strongly, he'd run haphazardly, bladder still screaming, into the darker part of the woods; only to find his Pa, directly in his path, sneering at him, and cuffing him none too gently around his ear, had dragged him back to the cart. He suffered for that, nearly a month had passed before the binds were released yet again, his food ration meagre the entire time. The second attempt, and the third, for that matter, hadn't gone much better.

Chapter 31 – 1959 – The Artifact

And so, the years had passed, and in a strange way, he was indoctrinated. He had become used to the travelling way, rising with the sun, foraging, cooking together over the camp fire. He supposed they had reached something of a begrudging truce, mostly. And then; then, they remained the longest they had ever stayed, anywhere.

For months now, they'd been camped just outside of the Romany site, near the river, watching. His Pa with fevered obsession, glared at the older man Po, tracking him as long as the light held good. Sometimes Ben had stirred at night and watched his Pa, seemingly mesmerised by the heart fire of the other camp, lying in the still night air, just watching. He'd seen him smiling ominously at the sight of the impassive and silent woman with the haunted eyes, Lylie. Daniel had watched almost gleefully, the man Tommo and the baby gal, approach her time and time again, always receiving no response. She was failing, even Ben could see that, and he had finally found out why.

The ramblings of his Pa, both while drunk and sometimes when crying out from his restless dreams, had filled in the small gaps that had been left out of Daniel's tales, and knowing like he did, his Mum's and Grandpa's dislike of him, how his Mum had been; her utter lack of emotion, her violent rejection of any physical contact, well, he had figured out the rest for himself, and he finally knew in his heart, that he wasn't far off the truth. Daniel had caused this.

He looked over at the man who lay still in the grass, the wasted body, the glittering, hate filled eyes, yes, he was to blame. Yet still, the man continued to believe that he was the one that had been wronged.

Ben had watched alongside his Pa, the night the Guardians were raised, their frantic efforts to reach Lylie, to save her. He'd been entranced by the ethereal figures, captivated by the astonishing scenes before him. Never in his life had he witnessed such a poignancy, such dedicated fervour, and he was awed.

And Rina, …somewhere in his chest something long dead had moved. She was beautiful, her hair, her eyes, her very soul. Even in her agony, and the months that had followed, waiting on her Mam, caring for the babe, cooking for the family and running the camp, she was everything in a maid that he had never thought a woman could be. He wanted her, more than anything in this lifetime, he just wanted her.

They visited the nearby town later that week. He was excited, it wasn't often he got the opportunity to hear the hustle and bustle of others, to listen into happy conversations, see the *Gorga's,* as his Pa derogatively called them, about their busy lives. Homes to go to, inside fires to attend, food on the table with maybe a tablecloth? They sounded happy, something he'd long aspired to.

Perhaps there'd be a young maid whose eye he could catch. He knew, if he took after his Pa, or how he'd used to look anyway, that he was probably easy on the eye too, and if Rina wasn't ready yet, well then, the possibilities were endless. He had no ties.

The streets were cobbled and busy like he'd hoped. His senses were inundated with colour, sound and smells. The raucous cries of the stall holders, the echoes of laughter, the odour of cooking. It was a balm for his battle-scarred soul.

They needed supplies, they were running short, so Daniel had begrudgingly left his vantage point that morning, grumbling and bad tempered, but he wouldn't *not* come, *probably felt he had to keep an eye on him.*

The stalls, rammed with vegetables, cheeses, eggs and all sorts of useless paraphernalia, called to him seductively, he had a few coins squirrelled away, maybe…

Daniel suddenly froze beside him, his eyes narrowing perceptibly. "Can't be, surely not …. No, can't be." He walked slowly, steps deliberate, ringing out, the sound of his hob nailed boots cutting clean across the din, over to a stall on the other side of the village street. As far as Ben could tell, the old boy who owned it, chatting to other browsers good humouredly, seemed to be wily, negotiating some fair sums for the scrap goods on the stall. He wasn't interested though, it looked far from enticing, dreary almost. Watches, old dark silver chains, broken cufflinks, *boring*, he thought, *come on Pa*. He shifted impatiently.

Daniel was approaching the stall holder, his face wreathed in an amicable smile. Ben hardly recognised him, and he knew that this unprecedented behaviour, so unlike his Pa, meant something important was afoot. And he wasn't going to miss it, oh no, not for all the tea in China. He ambled over, curiosity in every step.

"Let's see what you got 'ere then?" Daniel rummaged around on the stall taking his time, lifting and inspecting, turning and peering at several of the items on the tabletop. Ben could see his eyes darting elsewhere though, and guessed that his real interest lay in a different object. He was just playing the old boy.

"No, not today, I don't think, but I'll be back Mister, you got some good stuff rite enough," his Pa said eventually, turning to go, but then he stopped nonchalantly, almost absent-mindedly, to pick up a pocket watch on the front of the stall. "Look at that, it's just like my old Pa's." He smiled winningly at the man, "He's bin gone many a year, but 'tas taken me back that 'as." He sighed, putting the watch back on the tabletop sorrowfully. "I 'spec you want more than I got for that 'un, shame." Sighing heavily, he turned away, shoulders stooped.

"Hold on man," came the stronger than expected voice of the stallholder, "let's talk, no harm in that surely?" Daniel looked bleaker. "Mister I got what I got in this 'ere old pocket, nothing more, and me and the boy is supposed to be getting supplies. I wish it were different. Not this spell, you back 'ere agin sometime?"

"Look, how much you got?" the old boy muttered. "It's been a slow day, let's see what we can do for you, I got a heart you know!" Ben looked at the wily old man, almost raising his eyebrows, but managing to contain himself, looked away quickly, smirking.

Daniel scrabbled around in his waistcoat, scattering all his change onto the table, pulling his pockets inside out. "This is it, Mister, sorry to say, times bin hard. I understand, that you want more for this, and if I had it, I would part with it in a flash, reminding me of my old Pa like it does." He sniffed despairingly, "I haven't got it my friend, so I won't waste your time no more."

He started to gather the coins together, as the old boy, nodding his head, gave way to Daniel begrudgingly, knowing he'd been outmanoeuvred. There was a twinkle of respect in his rheumy eyes, "Go on my son, you fought a good fight, you win, take the watch."

"Dear God Almighty, 'tis a miracle," Daniel muttered striding and stopping, scrutinizing the old watch, turning it this way and that, pressing the spring on the side, clicking the watch open and peering hard. "'Tis it for sure, bloody hell's bells, who'd have thought!" Ben fought hard to tame his irritability, hands itching to shake some sense out of the man; his Pa had been like this for hours.

They'd reached the camp a while ago and still he paced, his muttering becoming more and more incoherent, yet with a trace of jubilation starting to build in his tone his usually churlish demeanour. He was almost engaging.

"'Tis it, Ben!" With astonishment, Ben stared back at him, grimly. *Ben*, he'd actually called him *Ben!* and with a sickening lurch he knew something unparalleled was occurring, and for the life of him, try as he might, he couldn't work out what that might be.

❖

Chapter 32 – The Present – Cottage

"It was the Time Piece. He found the Time Piece." Mum spoke into the silence of the room, her eyes hollow in her face. "Mum?" I questioned uneasily; she held up her hand. "My turn," she said firmly. "But I thought you said …." I faltered out, "that was then, darling," turning her head to the door said quietly, "Listen."

None of us needed to strain our ears, the howling gale outside, flung itself unnaturally at the stoic cottage door, pummelling and screaming, straining the old timber in its frame. "There's no time now, this has to be done." She took a breath.

'No one may enter,' I intoned to myself for the umpteenth time.

She looked at each of us in turn, Jon, his face immovable, stared back seemingly impassive, but the slight sheen glistening on his brow told me a different story. Dad broke in sighing, and catching her hand said, "Look," and he encompassed the newly knowledgeable girls in his gaze. "The Time Piece is a valuable object, *immensely* sought after, many people have travelled the length and breadth of the land searching for it over the decades, including our own families. Now, it's not valuable merely in terms of its physical worth," he paused, thinking how to explain sufficiently and as succinctly as he could. Lowering his head and thinking out loud, he continued, "It *is* similar to the Pendant, in the sense that it *is* extremely powerful. However, in the case of the Time Piece, well, it can only be used, at least to its *full* potential, in conjunction with the Pendant."

We waited; we were all aware that our voices were fighting the noise of the storm outside. In subliminal agreement, we acknowledged we were going to have to keep this brief, we had to move things along.

Binny, ensconced on one of the battered kitchen chairs in the corner of the room, raised her head. She took a deliberate sip of her full glass and staring hard at the ceiling said sagely, "And of course, we *all* know where the Pendant is, don't we?"

Thin lipped we nodded at each other, our faces strained, the others now showing signs of the fear that I had carried with me for so long. I rested my empty glass on the arm of the chair, twisting my body towards them, uncramping my legs, flexing them, gathering my thoughts. *How much vodka could you drink before it dulled the fear?* I gathered myself; we were here, right now, in this moment of time, and they all knew. My heart still sang with the knowledge that at last, I wasn't alone.

As I paused, almost ready to fill the tense silence, a voice came at me briskly, her face illuminated in the flickering fire light; "So, this is why you've been so bloody crabby then?" Elsie asked, her brows raised questioningly at me; *understatement of the year I thought,* almost, but not quite; smiling. "Someone is after the Pendant? Is that it? Is this what this is all about?" She flung out her arm, indicating the storm, Lorentree Cottage, the people surrounding her. We looked back at her, watchful.

"So … let's clarify; we're here, because someone is trying to get the Pendant, am I right, sis?"

A split second passed before Libby spoke, her voice calm, but all the more eery for it, "Or … it could be said of course, that we are all here, to *rescue* the Time Piece, and I guess," she said, her blue eyes unblinking, "that the winner takes all."

I swallowed heavily, looking at Mum and Dad, who were frozen in place, wordless and grey faced. "Yes," I said quietly, "to both of you; yes … that's why he's here, and … that's what he wants."

"Who?" the girls both said in unison. Binny put her head in her hands; "Bris, bloody Bris," she said, her voice muffled. "or should I say *Ben*, my *glorious* step brother is here; and he's here to collect."

Chapter 33 – 1959 – The Camp

Ben stumbled from the camp that night, crazy with a grief he'd never expected to feel, fury too, along with bone melting, *fear*. Pa, his Pa was gone, destroyed before his very eyes, the man's anguished face filled his mind, his cries reverberating through his ears, weakening his strength, stealing his reason. Sobbing he'd fallen to the ground, craziness was beckoning him, and he wondered if he were finally too broken to stave it off.

The thoughts tore through him; never again would they travel together, he'd never hear the rough voice chastising him, the odd chuckle of malice, the never-ending tales of bravado, he'd never share another fire or tend to the horses with the man who had formed the second part of his young life. He tried to breathe, he felt disjointed, *less* somehow. Of course, Daniel had been a tyrant, a mean tempered, ill-mannered cuss of a man, but he was his *Pa,* and that counted for something. Daniel had been the only real family he had ever had.

And with Pa gone, taken, *destroyed,* like an *animal;* he felt the last vestige of human compassion fly from his soul. It winged its way out of him, away into the cool blue ether, somewhere he knew he would never find it again, he knew, because he would never again allow himself to be the needy, ignorant, trusting *child* he had been.

And he recognised just who had stolen that soul, the person who had finally broken him, even after everything he had endured, and he knew her name. He knew her, and God how he now hated her.

Rina; Rina would pay, if it cost him his last wretched breath, if it took him the remainder of his useless, blighted life, she would pay. She, and all she held dear.

He sat, swaying in the dell, his arms hugging his body; although it brought him scant comfort. He had to go back, he knew he did, he had to get their stuff, gather their meagre belongings before the bastard Romanies; he chuckled to himself, *he was far more like his Pa than he had thought;* before they pillaged and stole *it*.

Oh, he knew all about the watch. The very last thing that Daniel had done right, was to *explain*, God alone knew why, but for the *first time ever*, his Pa had told him straight, and now he knew he needed the Time Piece. That blessed artifact, would take him on his journey, a journey of vengeance and recompense, and finally, when his debt was settled, he would be able to live the life that he truly deserved. *At long last.*

It was while he was gathering the things, that he took a moment to examine the camp in the distance. He needed to catch his breath, try and gather his strength, just for a moment. The day was bright and warm, the sun high, even so, the heart fire in the Romany camp sent ember motes into the still air, its flames flickering happily, mocking his misery with their blissful dance.

His eyes strayed to the space under the tree, thinking to see Lylie gazing listlessly into the distance. She wasn't there. Startled, he quickly scanned the others and for a moment, he couldn't place her anywhere. Suddenly, like a stabbing blade to his heart, he saw her, sitting in the midst of the excited group by the heart fire, her face etched in an ecstatic smile, as a young girl bounced on her knee squealing, her husband

Tommo, kneeling at her side, both of them gazing at the child in union of pure joy.

For a moment his gaze held, unbelieving, and suddenly realisation struck.

One life for another.

Daniel had paid the price for this woman, for her freedom from the demons that had haunted her for so long. Bitterness rose in him, and as he watched, spite oozing from his pores, Rina strode into view, Po at her side, her face a picture of such unbridled happiness, a look that he knew, would imprint itself on his mind for decades to come.

Such was his rage, his utter, bleak despair that he nearly cried out at the pain that coursed through his body.

He could no longer bear to watch but as he started to turn, Rina lifted her head and stared into his eyes. She knew he was there, *could she feel him*? He knew she couldn't really *see* him. She lifted her hands, as though to ward him off, and he watched her lips moving, her face holding a trace of what? Fear? Anger? Filled with a premonition of disaster, dread rising like a tide in his gut, almost crushing him, he rose unsteadily to bolt, and as he did so, he heard the distant cries of the rooks rising.

Chapter 34 – 1978 – Mauve

"Windows Mrs?" The young man stood in front of her, his smile wide, charming, and for a moment, she felt disarmed, before replying distantly, "Windows?", and feeling off balance somehow, had repeated vaguely, "Windows?"

He pointed at the bucket, placed on the front step at his feet, "I'm doing the rounds see, just askin' if you want yer windows done." She looked at him curiously; did she know him, he seemed …. He was delving into his pockets, searching for something, his russet hair springing back from his forehead. She was caught for a moment, a fragment of a thought wriggling in her mind, spiralling away before she could capture it. "I…" she said hesitantly, as she saw him pull, of all things, an ancient pocket watch, out of his overalls. "Well, I got time, so to speak", he said casually, glancing at the watch, "so I thought I'd ask, nice house Mrs…" He looked enquiringly at the door.

She gazed at him blankly, her feet planted firmly on the sitting room carpet, as she sat timidly on her pristine sofa; how had he got into the house, she couldn't remember inviting him in, she didn't know if she'd asked him to do the insides of the windows, *had she*? She supposed she must have.

"Michael, it's a lovely school, I've spoken to the Headmistress, Caitlin can start next week, it's the Convent, you know, at the top of the hill on the left." She perched on the edge of the kitchen chair, her eyes strangely bright as she gazed at her husband, still in his work suit. "Wouldn't it be lovely for her, to make new friends, and the curriculum sounds simply amazing." She paused, it was settled, she'd made a decision, and was strangely pleased, decision making was something quite unfamiliar to her. She tipped her head slightly, muddled and lost for a moment in her own confusion.

Her husband looked at her with raised brows, studying her, his eyes narrowed. Her clipped syllables still vibrated on his nerves, years after the elocution lessons she had hungered for. Well not *hungered,* that would be a *sentiment,* and let's face it, Mauve didn't do sentiment.

What on earth though? Since when had Mauve ever taken an interest in the welfare/happiness of their daughter. He gazed back at her, nonplussed. Oh, he loved his wife, no doubt about that, but even he had to admit that she was not an easy woman to live with. In fact, many times over the years, seeing their daughter rebuffed time and again, watching the impassive void that was his wife, glide through her life without an ounce of empathy for the child, with hardly *any* consideration for her daughter's wellbeing, he had asked himself, *why*? Why, he had the feelings he did for her.

"You enrolled her at a new school?" he exclaimed finally. "Really Mauve? Why on earth didn't you talk to me about it first? Does Caitlin know, is she happy about leaving her old school?" He gazed at her in disbelief; patently baffled, and finally, tentatively, with a degree of horror, "Does she even know, Mauve, tell me she knows?"

"Darling, really, what do you take me for? As it happens, I haven't actually spoken to Caitlin yet, but I do feel, *I really do*, that she will appreciate me taking an interest!"

"Mauve," he started, shaking his head slowly, frustration etched in the lines on his face. "Michael, really," she cut in with something close to exasperation, and even that small display of irritation, took the wind from his sails. "Do you have to make such a fuss? And now look, I have the most atrocious headache," she deadpanned, "you can chat to her later darling, tell her it's next week. Oh, and you'll need to get her a bus pass. Oh, yes, and a uniform, yes, a uniform, I hear it's brown." She sniffed vaguely, "I daresay that will be my fault too."

First class, first lesson, and she smiled at her across the classroom – Anna, the girl with the blond curls. She had to smile, Anna was off on another of her petit mals, gazing into the distance as though no one else existed. She'd been called out on it a couple of times already, but had smiled at Sister Dorothy, so disarmingly, that the elderly teacher had melted.

"Hey, I'm Binny," she said at break, squatting down beside her on the dry grass beside the courts, and Anna gazing back at her, blue eyes twinkling, had broken her biscuit in two and handed her half. "I know," she said, "odd name, but it suits you somehow," and they giggled together lost in the moment, for the first of very many times.

⊷⊶◄◆►⊷⊶

Chapter 35 – The Present – Lorentree Cottage

"Listen," I started, "Bris has been on my radar for a long time. You may think that this is new to me, and to Binny, but …" I looked at her and she nodded me on; "I thought I could deal with him. So …. anyway, it turns out I can't. Believe me, if I could have kept you out of this I would have." I looked at the girls in turn, meeting their gazes, and finding just more questions in their worried eyes, I turned to Jon. "Tell them the rest," I said bleakly. "But be gentle." He looked back at me a little reproachfully, "Of *course,* sis, but this has got to be blunt, it's not a fairy tale, no point in hiding anything anymore is there?" I shook my head wearily, "No I guess not, go on then, just do it."

"Bris needs the Pendant," he continued steadily, "he needs it to fully realise the potential of the Time piece. Without it, he's almost powerless, unless you count some fairly harmless magicians' tricks and petty conjury." He sniffed derogatorily, "Something and nothing really, but *with* the Pendant," he paused, troubled, "well things would be *really* different, then the real 'fun and games' so to speak, would begin. Can you imagine how powerful that man would be?

"We've already had a taste of his frustration, his rage, I can only imagine how much further he would go. Suffice to say … I think we wouldn't be given any opportunity to live our lives in harmony, or in fact, I hate to say it; but to … um … live our lives at all."

The silence in the room was leaden, a collective air of despair drifting its way through our senses, leaving us shocked and afraid. The fire hissed its ire, as the clock missed a beat. No one spoke. The only sound to break the silence was Dad moistening his dry lips, before topping his glass up.

"Now listen, the position we are in right now is this; Bris has threatened Anna, he has made his intentions clear; he is aware of the situation, he knows somehow, God alone knows how, that we all hold a quarter of the key." They all looked at me searchingly. I shook my head grimly not wanting to go into the details. It wouldn't help, not now. Jon looked at the girls, speaking to them directly; he knows he cannot take, by force, by manipulation or without full consent, any of the parts. But in *not* enabling him to achieve his goal, we are all in a terrible situation." He turned towards Binny and raising his eyebrows said, "All yours Binny, please go on."

"Okay," she said flatly "He has a plan, and I don't know what it is. God knows I've ... we've all, tried to work out his angle," she took in Jon, myself and Mum and Dad in her look, "but we just don't know how he hopes to achieve the seemingly impossible short of just finishing us all off! Even that wouldn't work, the Pendant would return to the Guardians if the hosts no longer existed, but obviously that's small comfort," she grimaced, "and it's not part of any plan we've tried to create, and that's all I can say really."

We looked at each other silently; *where do we go from here*? Terror stampeded its way further into the room.

She stumbled to a stop as the atmosphere in the room shifted slightly.

"Rose?" Mumbled Mum puzzled, and I nodded, "Yes, I feel her." I lifted the protection, just as a gentle knock sounded at the door. "Come in, come in," Mum called, a small smile lifting the concern from her face for just a moment. "Rose, darling, what are you doing here?"

Running slim fingers through her hair and shaking the rain from her face, Rose smiled gently into the room. "Helping of course, like I always said I would." She looked around the room, taking in the dim light, the fire flickering its welcome, and the sight of wine and cheese on the table.

"Did you think I would stay away? You know me better than that! Ah lovely, wine, yes please."

She brought the smell of summer with her, flowers and sunshine, dew on cut grass, and a gentleness of aura that encompassed us all. Her eyes shone with innocence and purity. Strange that the world and all its ills never seemed to reach out its callous tendrils and strangle that incorruptibility. Strange and wonderful.

Sitting on the last remaining kitchen chair, squeezed into the corner of the room, warming herself at the welcoming fire, she gazed at us serenely.

"Now family, it's my turn for the Pendant." She looked around calmly, "My turn to keep it, and you, safe." As we opened our mouths to utter the absolute rejection of the idea, of putting her in harm's way, she shut us down with a simple wave of her hand.

"No, my darlings, it makes sense, just listen.

"Bris is a monster," she looked at Jon lovingly, "look what he's already done to us. We're living in fear, and it'll go on, just like Gram said. Rina, you remember, *'it'll go on and on for the rest of time'.*" Mum nodded grimly, her knuckles white, and Dad reached across to grip her hand.

"But, if I take the Pendant, or at least all its parts, you give it to me willingly, all in agreement, he won't know where it is. Bris won't know. Only we, in this room will ever know. You see," she said calmly, her eyes shining, "he'll never know I was here. I came incognito," she paused "I came *quietly,* do you understand?"

"You cloaked?" Mum said questioningly? "Yes," she replied triumphantly, I *cloaked*!" The fire roared, and somewhere out in the stricken darkness a rook cawed its approval.

"You cloaked?" Elsie rasped out, "you mean, like invisible?" "Yes darling, just like that" she smiled. "I was *invisible.*"

"Bloody brilliant, Rose," Dad burst out, clapping his hands, "absolutely bloody brilliant, well bloody done." "Hear, hear," echoed Jon, as the rest of us gabbled in excitement, relief flooding through us.

"Hold on a moment everyone," Libby said, cutting into the chaotic jubilation, and somehow her calm voice reached us all, shutting us down, pulling trepidation back into the room by its coat tails. "Pardon me for putting a dampener on this fabulous offer," she stroked Rose's arm apologetically, "but isn't this just buying time? Bris isn't going to give up, he will track you down Aunt Rose, for *ever,* just like he has us, he's not stupid, this just delays things doesn't it, or am I missing something?"

"Oh darling, you *are* right to an extent, this is a delaying tactic. But look around you, you all *know.* All of us are in this together because now you *know*, and this time, we will plan, we will be ready, we will be strong." She looked around for acknowledgement as we nodded back at her, hope beginning to blossom again, just as Elsie spoke up, "Yes, you're right

Aunt Rose, this time we'll be ready," she looked around at our grim faces, "that bastards got it coming."

Chapter 36 – The Present – Lorentree Cottage

We waited. Sitting in the warmth, our fevered breathing filled the room with nervous energy. The storm outside grew stronger, its tormented frustration mounting, the noise was *unholy.* Were we the only ones to be afraid this night?

Listening to the pounding and thrashing, the wildness of the prolonged assault, we marvelled at the fury causing the onslaught, this frenzied attack, and we knew that however we got out of this, it was unlikely all, if any of us, would remain unscathed.

Five minutes to midnight, and with one accord, our gazes settled on the old clock. Its face seemed to freeze under the scrutiny, just for a second, and then it resumed, passing each tortured minute with sighs of defeated resignation.

It's not your fault, I sent silently: there's *nothing* you can do, just keep ticking old friend. The lined face glistened and for a moment sadness touched us all, caressed us with its sinuous hand, and we nodded back in acknowledgement and thanks, our old friend, Time, always there for us.

That very thought broke through my subconscious like a bolt of lightning. Time, our constant, our companion, our *friend.*

Looking at the clock through misty eyes, I smiled, and the old clock smiled back tenderly, "Thank you," I whispered hoarsely, *"thank you, old friend."*

The clock struck midnight, the reluctant chimes ringing through Lorentree Cottage, cutting the air, charging us with intent.

Just as the last chime tolled, the door flew open on its hinges, smashing into the wall behind, shaking us to the core as the night air flew furiously into the room, rain and wind lashing at us, swiping at our hair and plastering our faces with its freezing touch. The roar was monstrous, relentless and jubilant, we huddled there, each of us freezing and dishevelled, our fear filled faces watching the open doorway, portraying the effect of an evil portal, waiting for an archaic demon to show its malevolent hand.

"Show yourself, Bris," Dad suddenly shouted into the darkness, and standing sharply, he beckoned, his finger crooked, "well *come on* then, we're all waiting for the big reveal, all these intimidation tactics, and what, now you're shy?" He chuckled light-heartedly, seemingly amused. Mum looked up at him, fascinated; all those years together and he still had the power to surprise her. She shook her head in bewilderment, as the rest of us stared at him open mouthed: was this part of an undiscussed plan?

However, it seemed that surprise *had* gained him the upper hand, he'd taken control, for the moment at least, *he was buying time, for us.* The wind stilled in its howling, the rain pattering to a timid mizzle, the elements were confused, who was the *master* here?

A sinister figure materialised suddenly in the darkness of the open doorway, the low, trembling fire, picking out its features erratically. Moving shadows cast his face in an unsettling glow, highlighting the prominent cheekbones, emphasising the darkness of the hollows under his eyes and outlining his face much like a cadaver, causing us to draw in our breaths in communal horror.

"Well, hello, at last, Bris," came Dad's calm voice from the dimness, "it's been a while, how have you been?"

The forced camaraderie fell thinly into the now silent room. Bris paused for a moment, his eyes narrowing.

"Samuel," he snarled, "*now* isn't the time for small talk, that time has long passed. Let's face it, your choices are few and far between right now." He stepped into the room, as the door behind him thudded shut unwillingly, at the turn of his hand.

"Party tricks," Jon muttered just beneath his breath and raising himself, he too, stood tall beside Dad; their height and breadth diminishing the slighter form of the thin man in front of them.

Bris wasn't deterred, he smiled spectrally, arrogance shrouding him like a cloak, emanating from him with such force it was almost tangible. "Hand over the Pendant … now, *all* of it, all its parts." He looked around triumphantly, did he really expect praise for gleaning a little knowledge? Well, he wasn't going to get it from us, none of us spoke. He took in our careful, impassive faces, and glanced away, chagrin written clearly across his features. He held out his hand, upturned and ready. "Give."

"Dear boy," Dad said smiling, his voice saccharine, "the Pendant or '*any of its parts*' isn't *here* with us. The fact is," he turned to sweep his hand around us all, "we couldn't keep it safe." He smiled almost pityingly, "Did you think we would sit here and wait for you to come and *snatch* it from us, like a bully in the playground?" His voice hardened perceptibly, "It's gone Bris, gone from us, gone from this house, gone from this … world."

We eyed Dad surreptitiously, afraid, each one of us doubting, and terrified that his tactic, whatever it was, would work. Didn't he realise that he could leave us all wide open to vindictive and merciless consequences, if we were proved to be useless, empty vessels, with no Pendant part in any of us. The very fact rendered us dispensable, surely? But Dad continued on and we waited, watching the scene unfold, held in a thrall of horrifying anticipation.

Bris laughed derisively, low and chilling, and stepping further towards us, raised his hand. Clutched in his grasp, we could see the outline of the old watch, the Time Piece. "You know what this is?" he sneered. "It's the *Time Piece*. I don't need your empty, lying words, I've got the means to check for myself."

He lowered his eyes to the object, preparing to voice his command.

I suddenly caught the intense gaze of Elsie, '*look*' she sent, '*just look with your eyes, don't move your head.*' Her eyes shifted hard to the right, high on the wall. I moved my eyes instantly; and saw the hands quivering fretfully on the face of the old clock. '*What do you need old friend?*' The hands whirled around the old face, stopping at ten past three. *What? What did that mean?* Libby shifted her head imperceptibly, her eyes directing me. '*Move*' she sent, '*to ten past three of the room. **Now** sis!*' '*What, me move?*' '*clear Times path, quickly, go.....*' My mind was in a fog of fear, frantically the hands jiggled their agreement at me, '*Quickly, move to ten past three of the room!*' "*Go!*" the girls sent pithily.

'*Elsie, I can't! I need a distraction!*' Her face was an abrupt picture of utter absorption, but she didn't falter, not for a moment. I could see her sparring with doubt and then fear, and *then* the righteous fury hit, she was intent on her goal *thank God*!

'*Could she do this?*' She, who had practised no arts since they had been snatched from her at seven years old, and anyway, none of us knew what her gift actually was. *Did she even know herself?*

She raised her arms fiercely, her outstretched fingers pointing unwaveringly at Bris, and then the *fire* burst from her. The crackling, scorching and spitting heat, cut through the tense air, steadfast and merciless, in a huge wave of determined and glorious flame.

Her power was immense.

We were held motionless in our seats, mesmerised by the sight before us. Elsie standing tall and proud, firelight glancing off her face, her fingertips ablaze as she held her ground with seemingly effortless ease.

Dear God, she was a *Fire Witch*.

Coming to, from my momentary stupor, I leapt from my seat, staggering to stay upright on deadened legs, and threw myself behind Bris, just as the old clock tolled once more.

Bris startled backwards from the wall of flames, off balance, but not in retreat, oh no, he was furious. His face hardened as he compressed his lips into a thin line. *Please God let this work, or we'd be done for by the looks of things.* He looked to his hand once more, his lips starting to move, and at that moment the old clock called to the Time piece in a shard of light, reaching out to it, entreating the battered talisman in an ancient tongue:

'*My friend, my kin, your allegiance is sorely misplaced. Time is no enemy to those that hold the Pendant dear, to those of them that only serve in compassion, and who seek nothing in return. You are bidden now to return to us, to ensure forthwith that your power is used only in virtue, with no recompense. It is the will of the Pendant, and these are her children. Come child of mine, I call to you, make haste, there is little time to spare and we have much to accomplish before the dawn toll.*

Chapter 37 – The Present – Lorentree Cottage

Bris, his ears not tuned in, or maybe just oblivious to the clock and the conversation, held just moments ago in the language of the old tongue, uncaring perhaps of the plead of the ancient one; raised his voice to command the Time Piece.

The wind and rain, fretful of their alliance now, settled into the corner of the room, biding their time, like a pair of shamed puppies, quietly watching and waiting for reassurance.

We watched alongside them; God knows it was time to admit we had done all we could. *We were beaten*.

Elsie exhausted from her act, had staggered backwards and perched haphazardly on the edge of the sofa, breathless and choked with emotion, while Libby smoothed her arm, muttering gentle charms under her breath.

"Bris," Binny interjected heatedly, but he shut her down, with a curt, "Quiet!" and she subsided into a helpless silence, glancing at me brokenly.

"Time Piece, where is the Pendant?" he was triumphant, but now he held an empty vessel, there was no response from the ancient artifact, no vibration, or tune, no musical rejoinder. The Time Piece no longer resided within its shell.

We looked towards the old clock, hanging in silent dignity, its face reflecting the firelight.

Boom! An ear-splitting toll suddenly rang out, deep and resonant, thrilling in its strength of purpose, its dignity and pride. We shook with the power of the sound. The clock was magnificent; swelling and growing in front of our eyes, to many, many, times its usual size, radiant and pulsing with the new found vigour of a kinship reignited at the eleventh hour, a unison of family.

Boom! A second toll followed. *Two am?* We sat mesmerised, watching in awe, our faces showing the wonder of the moment, alongside the beginnings of a welcome relief, my legs trembled uncontrollably as I started to make my way back to my chair, to sink into its comforting embrace, surely now, this was ended, and we were safe?

A shrill scream suddenly, pierced the air. Jumping from our seats, we turned towards the back of the room. "*Rose*," Mum screamed panic stricken, fear pouring from her in waves, "darling, uncloak, *uncloak*! we need to see you. *Oh God,* Rose? *Oh God*!"

Bris lay on top of a slender, translucent shape on the floor, his hands clasped around the neck of the gentle woman beneath him, squeezing and choking the life from her fragile body. As we surged forward, a tangle of limbs and frantic disorder, a wall of viscous darkness forced us back roughly. "He's protected," I screamed, incoherent with grief, "we can't reach her ...." My voice dwindled to a sob; "Mum, *oh my God,* we can't *reach* her ..."

"Anna," roared Dad into the melee, his finger pointing straight at me, "raise the guardians, *now*, raise them, do it now!" Shaken, and terrified, I could hardly raise myself, but the old clock, grander and more powerful than ever before, spoke gently,

'Anna, be calm child, the Pendant is with us, and now we have the Time piece. Have faith, let us call aid from our family together.'

Strained and anxious, shaking with fear, I raised my hands to my ears in the childlike fashion I remembered from old, and together Time and I, intoned the spell of the Guardians, our voices joined in solemn unity;

'Elders I call to thee, Materfamilias, Seraphs, Old Souls and Guardians, approach our table, share our fire, for tonight we request your guidance. We beg you wake from your otherworldly sleep and grace us with your presence, allow us your instruction, for we find ourselves in dire need of your aid. Come wake, rise, sit with your people, lend us your counsel, we the Romanies call to you.'

'We answer your call our family.'

Chapter 38 – The Present Lorentree Cottage

"Does it really matter?" I said briskly. "Here or in Spain, a cocktail's a cocktail surely?" "You bloody heathen," Elsie spat out crossly, her face a picture of ire, "of course it sodding matters, beach or drizzle, sand or tarmac, Christ Anna, get a grip!"

Libby cut in gently, "Yep it matters, sis," she replied to Elsie, "but does it matter enough to leave Aunt Rose recuperating alone, without all of us?" "God, really? What do you take me for, Aunt Rose is *coming with us*, how many times, we're *all* going, I told you this last week!" Elsie huffed indignantly, "we need this, God knows, it's not like I'm asking you to *emigrate*." She pouted, "He's gone Anna, *gone*. It's no use you pretending that this is all about Aunt Rose. We know you can't believe it, but the Pendant, the Time piece and the Guardians, well let's face it, if they can't fix things then what bloody chance *have* we got?" She paused for a moment filled with a moment of uncertainty. "It is fixed, right?"

"Of course," I said hoarsely, "you saw what I saw, sis, don't mind me, I'm just slower catching up with the 'it's all fixed' thing'." I gazed back at her, my face a picture of calm, as my wayward stomach churned evilly. "Book it, sis, let's go holiday on a *beach*, with a *cocktail*. No sodding *drizzle*. Or *tarmac*," I added breezily.

'Oh God ... help us dear Lord.'

'Oh Gram, I wish I didn't know.'

The old wisdom trickled through my head, twirling and prancing in a macabre dance; words from my Gram, through

Gran, passed to me from Mum, and they chilled me to the bone. More secrets … how could I ever have believed I would be free?

'My chavvi, my babe, heed me, this will go on and on, throughout the generations, it is written...'

The End

Further titles by Anna Woodbridge

The Time Piece - Part Two

The Amulet - Part Three

Authors Note

Anna lives on the outskirts of Exeter with her partner Andy. Together they are in the process of rennovating an old cottage. Anna has two daughters and five grandchildren, together with her partner they have between them eleven grandchildren.

Anna is part of a large, close family and confesses unashamedly to using their personalities and quirks to add depth to the characters within the books.

Anna has been writing for many years, but had not until The Pendant, published her works.

The Pendant is the first of a trilogy, followed by The Time Piece and The Amulet.

www.ingramcontent.com/pod-product-compliance
Lightning Source LLC
Chambersburg PA
CBHW071303190726
48292CB00007B/2669